fe

&f

Also by Kate Elizabeth Ernest

Hope Leaves Jamaica
Birds in the Wilderness

for younger readers

Tricky Tricky Twins

KATE ELIZABETH ERNEST

festus & felix

Mammoth

To my People
(especially Grandfather)
and the Land

First published in Great Britain 1994
by Methuen Children's Books Ltd
Published 1996 by Mammoth
an imprint of Reed International Books Limited
Michelin House, 81 Fulham Road, London SW3 6RB

Reprinted 1998

Copyright © 1994 Kate Elizabeth Ernest

The right of Kate Elizabeth Ernest to be identified as author
of this work has been asserted by her in accordance with
with the Copyright, Designs and Patents Act 1988

ISBN 0 7497 2385 8

A CIP catalogue record for this title
is available from the British Library

Printed in Great Britain
by Cox & Wyman Ltd, Reading, Berkshire

Contents

Foreword

At the beginning of the twentieth century education was not compulsory in Jamaica. Only the children of the middle classes enjoyed a good education. Then came the 1930s which were said to be 'turbulent years' in the West Indies: there were strikes and riots because social conditions were appalling.

The unrest of the 1930s was a turning point in Jamaica's history; two political parties emerged: the People's National Party and the Jamaica Labour Party. Universal adult suffrage came in 1944. The people had a voice. But it was not until the 1960s, after Jamaica gained her independence from England, that education became compulsory. Children from rural backgrounds, who studied hard, could take the Common Entrance Examination and gain scholarships to secondary education. Most parents and grandparents, who had received a basic education under the colonial system, were anxious for the future generation to move on; the promise of a scholarship was something to strive for. The story of Festus and Felix begins in 1964.

1

Jumping the Broom

It was a hot day and Felix, my best friend, had come down to my house carrying a message from his brother Osman, addressed to my sister Matilda. Mother was sitting on the verandah sketching a hummingbird which was buzzing round the poinciana tree in our yard. The tree was in bloom and there were red blossoms on the grass. Felix handed me the note and rushed off home. He avoided my father, who was standing on the verandah next to his mother, Granny Una, who lived with us. They were listening to the radio. Martin Luther King, the civil rights leader, had just won the Nobel Peace Prize.

'Let's hope this black Moses can lead his people to the promised land,' Granny Una said.

'Mm,' Father mumbled. 'Festus, what have you got there?'

'A note for Matilda, Father,' I said.

'More trouble.' Mother sighed.

There was a lot of botheration going on in our family. Messages were sent to my house via Felix, and I was the bearer of messages to Felix's house: my sister Matilda and Felix's brother were courting. Osman had recently sent Matilda a tiny bottle of perfume and a note. Father had intercepted the parcel and the note. He was angry. But later that day Osman came and sheepishly asked for Matilda's hand. Father soon calmed down. He said Osman was mannersable, though he still fretted about the match. He'd said it was all very well the two families being friends, being related was a different matter. Now he stood on the verandah saying to Mother, 'Lois, what would Papa Cuffee say if he were here now? African and Asian blood shouldn't mix.' (My people were ex-slaves who had acquired land after emancipation and Felix's people were a mixture of Chinese and Indian, who had come to Jamaica as indentured labourers during the 1840s.)

'Ah, Salvan,' Mother said. 'The old days are gone, dead and buried with the old people. Fancy sending Matilda perfume, sweet boy. We'll have to give them an acre of land, Salvan.'

Granny Una was sitting on the verandah with us. She said, 'Not ober me dead body, Lois. Me poor Cuffee would turn ober eena 'im grave if he know wat happenin.' Matilda will haffe go an' live wid 'er in-laws; dat's how yuh started married life.'

'Just a quarter of an acre, Salvan,' Mother said. 'Married people shouldn't have to put up with in-laws.'

'All right,' Father said. 'But not an inch more. That land belongs to Barnaby and Festus.'

'Salvan!' Granny Una snapped. 'Dat land belongs to de male line of de fambily: Barnaby an' Festus, yuh 'ear me?'

'I hear you, Mama.' Father glared at Mother. 'It won't harm Matilda to live with her in-laws for the time being.'

Usually, Mother got on well with Granny Una. But right now they were no longer on speaking terms. Mother snapped at Father, 'I wish your mother wouldn't keep interfering, Salvan. We'd better go and see Osman's parents now!' She flounced off.

Mother and Father went to see Felix's parents. It was agreed that Matilda would live with her in-laws; the wedding was arranged, and there were no bad feelings since Matilda liked Missis Leena, who was a seamstress. Matilda also loved dressmaking. She had attended homecraft school where she learned needlework and housekeeping. Matilda was a big-boned girl with her hair in two plaits, twisted across her scalp. She was dark-skinned with a gap between her front teeth. She was an average-looking girl. She always wore flat shoes and calf-length skirts, a bit like Mother really; they were both old-fashioned.

Having graduated from homecraft school, Matilda was unemployed for several months, and during that time she helped Missis Leena out, hemming dresses. That was how she had got to know Osman. Eventually she got a job in another parish, St Mary, keeping house at a Catholic mission. One day she found the priest dead in the bathroom; he'd died of a heart attack, calling out her name. Even though the new American priest wanted her to stay on, she returned home after the funeral. She could not forget Father Duffy's death cry. She said the place was haunted. Mother was adamant that Matilda should stay home until she found a position as housekeeper for a young head-master or a pastor, a responsible bachelor who was looking for a wife. That was what Mother had hoped for. She was secretly disappointed with Matilda for choosing Osman.

I never knew Matilda really. She was twelve years older than me, and because she'd been away at school and worked out for a while, she seemed so distant. She had travelled, left the village; other girls held her in awe. She had lived and worked with real Americans. She had acquired a certain amount of manners. She ate slowly, always telling me off. She spoke slowly, telling me to slow down. I tried to speak slowly, but I never could; not like Matilda.

Matilda had no friends. She lived in her own world.

11

But she got on very well with Missis Leena. She was to make the wedding dress and the two bridesmaids' dresses.

When I arrived at Felix's house Matilda was there for a fitting. There was red, patterned linoleum in the lounge-diner. There were patchwork cushions on a rickety sofa, and there was a plastic, patterned tablecloth covering the dining table. Faded photographs of their Indian and Chinese relatives hung on the wall. Like most of the houses in the village, there was a wooden, glass-fronted cabinet displaying tall glasses which were decorated with fruits, china saucers, and cups without handles. It seemed every house in the village had inherited chipped, hand-me-down china and fancy patterned glasses. Granny Una had offered hers to Matilda because Mother would one day inherit Aunt Hetty's heirlooms.

Matilda was wearing a gingham dress. Her hair was hidden under a headtie. She stood in the lounge-diner, holding the puffed-sleeved white dress which Missis Leena had been working on. There were tiny white beads on the bodice. Matilda kept saying, 'Are you sure this dress is finished, Mother?'

I narrowed my eyes, surprised; Matilda was acting as if Missis Leena was already her mother.

Missis Leena kept saying to the two flower-girls present, 'Mek sure oono nuh 'tep 'pon de hem of me daughter-in-law's dress. Me noh want de skirt comin' weh from de blouse.'

'I thought you said it was finished, Mother?' Matilda said.

'A tuck 'ere an' a pin dere,' Missis Leena said. 'Whoop, bam, it finish. A noh yessiday me sewin' yuh know, daughter.'

The two flower-girls were called Marigold and Primrose. They were always in demand as bridesmaids because they were identical twins, and very pretty. They had little oval-shaped faces, big dark eyes and smooth ebony skin. Their hair was thick and always worn in two fat plaits with stiff ribbons sticking out. They tried on their yellow chiffon dresses with white crinolines peeping out at the hems. They were to wear wreaths in their hair, made with yellow and white flowers.

'Just think,' the twins giggled. 'Festus and Felix are going to be brothers-in-law.'

'Yuh bwoys couldn't get any closer.' Missis Leena talked with a pin in the corner of her mouth. She was putting a pin here and a tuck there, altering the twins' bridesmaid dresses.

Felix and I digested the fact, smiling. We didn't talk to the girls because we couldn't tell them apart. We attended the same school but they were in the year below us. We never ever talked to them because boys and girls each had their own territory in the school-yard. We wandered off, smiling proudly, saying, 'We are going to be brothers-in-law.'

The wedding reception was to be held at our house. Father had insisted on paying for everything. But Mas Rupee, Felix's father, wouldn't hear of it. He insisted on paying for the liquor: white rum.

The church was decorated with yellow and white flowers. There were so many people that some had to stand outside, and peep through the windows. The pastor's shoes squeaked as he rocked on his heels. Then the organ sounded and the service began. Mother sat erect, smiling. She wore white gloves, a white hat and a floral dress. Father wore a dark suit, so did Mas Rupee. Missis Leena wore a straight yellow dress with two side pockets and a kick-pleat at the back. She sat twiddling her toes and wincing in a pair of black stiletto-heeled shoes.

'If anyone knows of any reason why these two should not be joined in matrimony . . .' The pastor dragged out the words.

Aunt Hetty sat up front wearing an ancient, starched white dress and lace-up, creased, whitened shoes with little heels. She took a Chinese-style fan from her black patent handbag, snapped it shut. 'Lawd, Pastor, noh baddah put temptation eena peeple way. Skip all dat nonsense an' get on wid de ceremony!'

Matilda and Osman made their vows. Osman was really nervous. He said, ' . . . and dereto I plite my traff.'

'Traff, what kind of traff?' Felix knitted his brow.

'I think he means a water trough,' I said.

Aunt Hetty fanned herself. (She was in her eighties and she was Mother's grandmother. Her son Benjamin, Mother's father, went to Costa Rica seeking work when Mother and her twin brother Uncle Ezra were born in 1928. He never returned home. Their mother died of consumption in 1930, so Aunt Hetty took the children as the rest of Mother's family had emigrated to Panama in the 1900s.) She said: 'Young man, speak a little better: yuh not plightin' yuh trough to de young lady; you are plighting your troth!'

The younger children giggled. The pastor coughed. The adults kept a straight face and the elders nodded. 'Mm.'

Osman wore a dark suit. He was well built with dark curly hair. He repeated: 'And thereto, I plight my troth . . .'

Matilda chewed her bottom lip. The service ended without further interruption. The choir sang 'All Things Bright and Beautiful'. Then Father took Matilda's hand and gave it to Osman, saying, 'Young man, good things come to those who wait.'

'Amen,' the congregation agreed.

The flower-girls kept their distance from Matilda's hem, clutching their yellow and white posies. They stood behind her, smiling. People tried to keep a straight face when Aunt Hetty tapped her walking-stick on the polished floor and declared: 'Young people, a wish yuh 'ealth, strength, 'appiness: first a girl an' secon' a bwoy!'

We had expected the pastor to have the last word. But no one seemed to mind. Aunt Hetty's blessing was important. She was not only the eldest in the village, she was still the storyteller and had been the village midwife, so she'd presided over Osman and Matilda's births.

Back at our house, a booth had been built in the yard. It was good to see the red blossoms from the poinciana tree strewn all over the grass. The humming-birds were out in full. Inside the booth, a buffet table was laid: fruit, a large hard-dough bread shaped like a duck, sandwiches, sorrel wine, sweets, fried chicken, coconut cakes, meat balls... There was curried mutton 'n' rice on the boil in the kitchen. Mother and Missis Leena had everything under control. Everyone admired the huge heart-shaped cake which Granny Una had made in an old kiln: the cake was decorated with blue and pink petals.

Matilda and Osman cut the cake. Food was served on paper plates and after everyone had eaten, Mas Rupee took Osman's hand and gave it to Father. 'Salvan, yuh gainin' a son and me gainin' a daughter; de pickneys kill de old hatred with love.'

'Welcome to the family, son.' Father shook Osman's hand.

Matilda and Osman seemed to have lost their tongues. They just kept smiling. In fact, our parents seemed to enjoy their wedding more than the bride and groom. They did all the talking, mainly about old times; love conquering hatred.

The pastor presented Matilda with a broom. 'New broom sweeps clean.'

Aunt Hetty had been sitting in her rocking-chair which had been brought down from her cottage. She sat under the poinciana tree, saying: 'Pastor, yuh is a real traditionalis'. Me neber thought me would live fe see de old tradition revive.'

The pastor took the broom from Matilda and held it high. But it was too high for her and Osman to jump over. Then he lowered the broom, and it was too low for them to crawl under. Everyone applauded the drama and joined in singing:

'Here we sit like birds in the wilderness,
Birds in the wilderness . . .
Lord, rock my soul.

It is so high that you can't get over it,
Can't get over it . . .
Lord, rock my soul.

It so low that you can't get under it,
Can't get under it . . .
Lord, rock my soul.'

After the sing-song ended, the pastor lowered the broom: 'Come, my children; jump the broom.'

Osman and Matilda held hands and jumped over the broom. Then the elders said: 'Our people used to jump the broom in the old days; that was before Christian marriage was introduced by the missionaries.'

One of the elders had a banjo. He began to play a catchy tune and Aunt Hetty was fired up. She sang:

'Under de poinciana tree we mus' be,
Like blackbuds in a nest.
Osman, rise an' stand up on yuh legs
An' choose de one dat yuh love de best.

Matilda, when yuh married a wish yuh joy,
First a girl an' secon' a boy.
Seven days after an' seven days to go,
Brek'fus give unto you.

Den you wheel 'er to the right
An' wheel 'er to de lef',
Wheel 'er to de right an' to de lef' . . .
Give 'er a kiss an' send 'er away . . .'

Aunt Hetty encouraged Osman and Matilda to dance. Osman wheeled Matilda to the right and to the left. Mas Rupee spun Missis Leena round and round while Mother and Father followed suit. It was a joyous occasion. Felix and I found ourselves spinning the flower-girls round and round, all singing: 'Den yuh wheel 'er to de right an' wheel 'er to de lef' . . .'

When the merrymaking ended, Granny Una took both sets of families aside. 'Children, marriage signify de joinin' of two fambily an' as 'ead of dis fambily, I expect fe have de las' word at all times; yuh 'ear me?'

'Yes, Mama . . . Granny,' we chanted.

2

The Quadrille

Education was something my parents took seriously when I was a boy. Every evening, on weekdays, I had to do homework. My parents were adamant that I would not work the land. Grandfather Cuffee had known real history, knew all about Africa, the Backras, but he couldn't read and write; he only went to basic school. He had to help his father on the land, and when my father was born in the 1920s there was land but no money to finish his education. Grandfather Cuffee made Father promise solemnly that at least one of his children would get an education. All hopes were pinned on me because Barnaby and Matilda had taken little interest in their schoolwork.

Mother stood on the verandah sketching a humming-bird, while I sat reading all about the Spanish conquest of the West Indies under Christopher Columbus, followed by the English conquest: General Venables and Admiral Penn. I also had to read about the kings and queens of England. I was really bored with it.

'Mother,' I said, 'where did the quadrille come from?' I had asked the question once before, but Mother had not answered me. She only shrugged.

'De quadrille was brought to Jimaica in seventeen something by de colonials,' Granny Una said. 'Now give yuh maddah a chance fe finish 'er sketch; let 'er ears eat grass.'

Mother remained silent. She admired her sketch proudly. She and Granny were firm friends again. She said without looking up, 'That's news to me, Mama. I never knew where the quadrille came from, never thought of asking you.'

'Yuh'd be surprised how much me know, Lois,' Granny said. 'Me went to all-age school right up to third grade, chile.'

Felix arrived, saying: 'Morning, Missis Lois; morning, Granny Una. Mama said to say howdy.'

Felix and I left Mother and Granny. We went to see Father who was standing outside the barn, milking a cow. Our dog, Buster, was standing next to Father. He was a huge black dog, the size of a cow-calf. He began to growl at Felix, playfully. The smell of lemon grass lingered in the air. Father was a big man who'd been known to trip over a pail of milk occasionally.

'Father,' I said, 'when will Felix and I be old enough to dance the quadrille?'

He looked up. 'Not now, Festus. I'm just about to milk Betty. I woke up late this morning and now I doubt if I'll catch the milk van. I don't want my milk money to be short.'

Father had several cows which he milked at dawn, taking the milk in a large aluminium bucket up to the village square; it was collected in big churns and taken to the condensary where it was turned into condensed milk. He ignored us, so we decided to go down to the river where the village women were doing the washing. Missis Leena's only sister, spinster called Aunt Rachel, was there too. She was a skinny woman whose black hair was littered with grey hairs.

'Howdy-do, Aunt Rachel,' Felix said. 'When will Festus and I be old enough to dance the quadrille?'

Aunt Rachel snapped. 'When your'e old enough, bwoy.'

Felix said impatiently, 'But when will that be?'

Aunt Rachel soaped the collar of a khaki shirt, grumbling: 'Yuh bwoys too carefree: idle donkeys always lead to pound . . .'

The women all wore sleeveless cotton dresses: thin arms, fat arms were exposed to the sun. Perspiration settled on their foreheads as they beat the washing on stones. A multitude of bubbles floated in the water and the sound of crips, crips, crips, could be heard as a combination of soap, air and material got caught up between their hands. Meantime stray hens searched for insects by the waterside.

'Eh-heh!' the women cackled. 'Is why yuh bwoys want fe rush thru life, tu'n man overnite?'

Felix and I lost our tongues there and then, overcome with shyness. We hastily left the waterside and went to see my brother Barnaby, who was feeding the pigs in the sty. The large black pigs were squealing and jumping over each other to get at the trough. Barnaby was wearing soiled denims tucked into wellingtons. He was thirteen years old. He had recently left school to help Father on the farm. He hated school. He was lanky and his clothes stuck to his skin. He picked up a stick and mixed the swill round in the bucket, ignoring us.

'Barnaby,' I said, 'when will Felix and I be old enough to dance the quadrille?'

Barnaby put down the aluminium bucket. He threw back his head and laughed. 'The quadrille is not for small boys. Go away. I'm busy just now.'

Felix and I left. We were glad to escape the squealing, grunting pigs and the smell of pig's swill.

'Let's go and see Osman.' Felix kicked up gravel.

Osman was chopping firewood with a cutlass. He wore dungarees and gumboots. His hair was full of wood chips. There was firewood all around, waiting to be bundled up.

'Osman,' Felix said, 'when will Festus and I be old enough to dance the quadrille?'

Osman put down the cutlass. 'When you're old enough to do men's work!' He wiped perspiration from his forehead with the back of his hand. 'Go away. Can't you see I'm busy?'

'Let's go and play cricket,' Felix said.

'OK,' I said. 'But we'll have to avoid Mother and Granny. They'll lecture me about doing schoolwork instead of playing.' At eight years old I didn't realise the importance of education; I only knew I had to do well in school because the family expected it of me. Secretly, I just wanted to be like other boys: sail kites, toss marbles.

'I'll race you.' Felix went running.

Three months after Osman and Matilda got married Aunt Hetty threw a party in their honour; they were adults now. Once again, Felix and I were curious about the quadrille. But everyone said we were too young to join in.

At dusk, on a Saturday evening, several of the villagers passed our house. 'Evenin', Mas Salvan, evenin', Missis Lois; see yuh up at Aunt Hetty's 'ouse later on.'

Mother was busy getting dressed. Father kept saying, 'Yes, breddas, catch you later.'

Felix and his parents arrived at last; everyone said howdy. Felix was staying at my house for the night. Granny Una would be keeping an eye on us. Father was fiddling with a torch and Mas Rupee said: 'Cho, Salvan, is moonshine tonite; yuh dohn need noh flashlight.'

Missis Leena told Felix to be good. Mother came out on to the verandah wearing a long plaid dress with a white puffed-sleeved bodice and white petticoat. Her hair was hidden under a plaid headscarf and there were lots of silver bangles on her wrists. She wore a string of wooden beads round her neck.

'Lois, gal,' Missis Leena said, 'wat a way yuh look like yuh 'oldin' up tradition!'

'National costume.' Mother laughed. 'Miss Lou's style. The quadrille is our national dance; you've got to dance it in traditional costume to capture that old-time feeling.'

'Yuh right, gal.' Mas Rupee took in Missis Leena's blue chiffon dress. 'Yuh mus' 'memba dat next time, Leena.'

There was no use Felix and me protesting. Our parents lectured us about behaving ourselves for my granny. Then they said good night and strolled down the path.

Father could be heard saying, 'Where's Osman and Matilda?'

'Dem wanted to walk alone,' Mas Rupee said. 'Never see two young people so shy. Anyway, dem soon get ober dat.'

Granny Una was a retired higgler. She used to ride her donkey, Baa-Baa, with its hampers loaded with yams, cassavas, gungo peas, cho-chos and pumpkins, several miles to the market in the capital of our parish, St Ann's Bay. We sat on the verandah, talking to her. She was a small wiry woman. As usual she was wearing a cardigan and socks as she was always cold.

'Tell us the story of the rolling-calf, Granny,' we said.

Granny Una loved telling us about the time when she and a few higglers were returning home from the market in St Ann's Bay and Baa-Baa became lame so they settled down by the roadside for the night. It was very dark and they were a long way from home. They decided to cook supper in a billy-can by the roadside.

They sang, 'Evening time, work is over; now is evening time . . .'

'Clink, clink . . . chains rattled in de distance.' Granny Una laughed. 'An we hollered: "Lawd a macy; rolling-calf ketch us now." De billy-can of food knock ober an' we huddle togedda, frighten outa we wits. We taut it was a duppy. But me.' She thumbed her chest. 'Me neber frighten, yuh know. Me just stan' me groun' an' seh, "Get dee behind me, Satan!"'

'What happened next?' we asked.

'We fall on we knees, praying: "De Lawd is my shepherd, I'll not want . . . Yea, though I walk thru de valley of de shadow of death, I'll fear no evil . . ." Den a cow-calf approached us, rollin' 'im big yeyes, mooin', an' dere was a chain rattlin' round 'im neck. No duppy, jus' a calf.'

Felix and I laughed until Granny Una sent us off to bed. She, too, went off to bed. We settled down until we heard Granny snoring. Then we crept out of the house and climbed the winding pass, hearing rustling in the bushes. We were nervous about being caught, but we were excited because we sensed that tonight we were about to witness the quadrille.

'Wild pigs,' whispered Felix.

There was a full moon and the trees cast shadows on the ground. We huddled closer together because we were afraid of the duppies. When we reached the top of the hill we heard the beat of the drums, getting closer and closer as peeny-wallies danced before our faces. We climbed a large star-apple tree, spying on the adults. They were all wearing their best clothes and there was not a cutlass in sight. The dancers stood in pairs, facing each other in a circle. They placed their hands on their hips and began to dance and sing: 'Dis long time, gal, me never see yu . . .'

The dancers shook hands with their partners, made

the movement of crows picking the blossoms off the tree top. Then they shook hands with their partners again, opened their arms wide and shook their heads. They stood in pairs, holding hands as they walked four steps clockwise round the circle . . .

'That must be the quadrille, Felix,' I said.

But Felix did not reply; he was trying to stifle a sneeze. The drums stopped beating and the dancers went off to refresh themselves, eating curried mutton 'n' rice and drinking coconut water; we could smell the scent of curry from where we were hiding. The drums rolled once again and we held our breath: Matilda and Osman stepped forward and the voices chanted:

'Moonshine tonight, come mek we dance an sing,
Moonshine tonight, come mek we dance an sing.
Me deh rock so, yu deh rock so, under banyan tree . . .'

'They're dancing the quadrille!' Felix sneezed. All eyes turned in our direction. We climbed down and our bodies shook as if we had the ague, we were in big trouble now. The adults came forward and fixed accusing eyes on us.

'But see yah, a couldn't me bwoy dat!' Missis Leena said.

Felix trembled when Mas Rupee exclaimed, 'Tan tuddy, bwoy. Yuh mean fe seh yuh disobey yuh maddah an' me?' He grabbed Felix by the scruff and marched him down the hill while my parents and I followed in silence.

When we arrived home Father said, 'Festus, off to bed! I will deal with you in the morning.'

Next morning I woke early but Father was already up. Granny was up early, too. She yawned. 'De likkle

24

scamps dem creep out w'en me fall asleep: rude and outa order bwoys.'

'But, but . . .' I said.

'Not another word in English, chile!' Granny Una snapped.

We were all standing on the verandah, watching the mist rising on the hillside. The dew had settled on the poinciana tree. As the sun came up over the hill, the dew glistened on the grass like diamonds.

Mother said, 'Festus, the quadrille is the only thing we have left over from the old days. When young people come of age, like Osman and Matilda, they join the rank of adults by dancing the quadrille. It means they are adults now.'

Father said: 'Festus, you and Felix are too inquisitive.'

'We won't do it again, Father.' I swallowed saliva.

'Too right,' he said. 'Disobedient children should feel the rod of correction.' He clasped his hands behind his back and watched the dew-water on the grass. 'Children grow up so fast nowadays.' He sighed. 'In my day you couldn't disobey your elders without getting the rod of correction.'

'Too right,' Granny Una said. 'Too right.'

'No harm done,' Mother said. 'The quadrille will probably die out with Aunt Hetty; just as well you got a glimpse of it.'

'True, true,' Father said. 'But disobedient children must be punished. You'll take over Barnaby's job in the pigsty today. I want him to run an errand for me.'

Monday morning, in the schoolyard, Felix and I examined each other for bruises. We had been spared the rod. Father had sent Barnaby with a note, asking Mas Rupee not to chastise Felix. We sat on the grass, recalling the adults staring at us wide-eyed, as if we'd caught them misbehaving.

'Look, Festus.' Felix pointed to a skinny boy

bopping, holding a pocket radio. All the children gathered round the boy, dancing and singing along with the radio: 'Ska, ska, ska, Jamaican ska; everybody come do de ska . . .'

Bap! The quadrille had gone out of fashion, just like that; everyone preferred the informal ska. Felix and I cried out of sheer frustration.

3

Freedom and Friendship

Felix and I were pleased when the annual Sunday-school outing came round because nobody would be dancing the ska that day. We felt silly moving our arms up and down, trying to do the ska. Anyway, the Sunday-school outing was organised by the pastor, his wife Sister Myrtle and the Sunday-school teacher, Sister Martha. We children boarded the bus noisily, holding our bankras or bags with our lunches. Meantime, the driver, an elderly man with several teeth missing, looked as if he was about to fall asleep. Our parents waved goodbye. Then the bus moved off and we sang, 'Kookaburra sits in the old gum tree . . .'

Sister Myrtle looked out the window at a flock of gulls, saying: 'Children, it is a sin to see the beauty of the countryside and ignore it. Look at God's handiwork.'

Felix and I were so used to the countryside, we took it for granted. When we looked we were surprised at the amount of fruits growing wild on an old colonial property: there were tamarind trees, mango trees, avocado-pear trees, banana trees, almond trees, all bearing fruit. As the bus jolted along, we observed cotton trees, fig trees, flame trees where hummingbirds and parakeets congregated, making a riot of colours. There was even a rainbow dipping into a pond where cattle, with gulls picking ticks off their backs, drank water while horses grazed, flapping their ears in annoyance.

Sister Myrtle was wearing a pastel-blue dress and a white turban. She was plump and her breathing was audible. Felix and I watched her pursed lips; there were lines at the corners of her mouth. She smiled at us. 'Boys, wherever you go in life, never stray far from the countryside: peace, perfect peace.'

We nodded. Sister Myrtle did not expect a reply.

We arrived at Dunn's River Falls where Felix and I stared at tourists. One of the tourists spoke to Felix in Chinese and Felix looked confused. He was upset because he couldn't understand what they were saying. They took photographs of him, saying: 'Jamaican Chinee . . .'

'I'm half-Chinese and half-Indian,' Felix said, 'and I can't even speak Chinese or Hindi. I only know how to speak English. I'm all mixed up. I hate myself and my parents.'

'Felix,' I said, 'you mustn't ever say that. It's not their fault, it's all because of slavery; we're all mixed up.'

'Boys, boys.' The pastor interrupted us. 'Manners. Stop staring at the tourists. It's time to climb the falls.'

We formed a human chain, with a Rastafarian guide leading the way. The pastor followed, wearing rolled-up trousers and bare feet. Sister Martha, who was as thin as a rake, walked in the middle, wearing a white turban and a floral, sleeveless dress. She wore yellow plastic shoes, pixies; so did Sister Myrtle, who commanded the children from the back.

Climbing the falls was like climbing up wide, giant steps hewn out of a mountainside where palm trees and wild flowers grew on one side, bending in the direction of the falls. The warm water rushed over our feet, sending swirls of bubbles past, on its way down to the sea. The rocks were slippery and Felix and I held hands tightly, supporting each other.

'Felix,' I said, 'suppose I fall? I can't swim.'

'You'd better not,' Felix said, 'because I'll come

28

tumbling down, too, and we'd both be washed down to the sea.'

The pastor calmed our fears by reciting all the way up the falls, ignoring the tourists. He said the falls reminded him of a long-forgotten poem, 'The Song of a Blue Mountain Stream' by Reginald Murray. We had also learnt the poem at school, and we recited eagerly:

'In a cleft remote
Where white mists float
Around Blue Mountain's Peak
I rise unseen
Beneath the screen
Of fog-clouds dank and bleak . . .'

'You'd be surprised wat dis falls cause peeple fe do,' the Rastafarian guide said. 'Som' peeple sing, some pray, some mek-mek, some laugh; but a neber 'ear poetry before. Mus' be de rushin' wata, sounds like music to de ear.'

Our next stop took us to a cave called Green Grotto Lake. We got out of the bus and queued up at a kiosk where the pastor bought our tickets. The bus-driver stayed with the bus. There was yet another Rastafarian guide. He led us towards the entrance of a limestone cave, shining a torch. He, like all Rastafarians, worshipped Emperor Haile Selassie I of Ethiopia, the Messiah, whom he said was descended from Solomon. He hoped that one day the Messiah would organise a mass exodus of black people back to Africa, the promised land.

'I thought Africa was the dark continent,' Felix said.

'Shush,' I whispered. 'The guide is listening.'

The tall ebony-skinned guide looked as if he'd been

carved out of mahogany. He had a staff strapped
across his back. He handed the torch to the pastor,
saying, 'De light of de worl'.' Then he walked with
the aid of his staff, which had a lion's image engraved
on the head. He patted it, adding: 'De lion of Judah,
rod of Jesse.'

Felix and I lingered behind, staring at the odd rock
formations. There was even a rock shaped like the
Virgin Mary holding a baby. There were spotlights
lighting the way. Ratbats squeaked and darted around;
we held hands really tightly, scared of the busy little
creatures.

'You boys should try to make friends with the other
children.' The pastor stopped. 'You can't live for
yourselves alone. What will you do when you have to
take separate roads in life, what then?'

Felix and I had taken it for granted that we would
always be together. We simply couldn't imagine
parting, not ever. We quickened our steps, though we
didn't join the other children. We wanted no other
company.

'Felix,' I said, 'I'm scared. Are you?'

'I want daylight,' Felix said. 'Suppose we lose our
way? We'd be trapped here for ever.'

'Lively up yourselves, children,' the guide said. 'Dis
is Arawak territory you're walkin' on, hallowed
ground.'

The roof of the cave seemed to be pressing down
on us, oppressive and humid. Each step took us
uphill. The path was smooth where thousands of feet
had trampled. Finally we started going down, down,
towards an indigo lake where the guide said blind fish
lived.

'Look, look.' The children pointed. 'More ratbats . . .'

There were numerous ratbats hanging from the

jagged ceiling of the cave. They squeaked and flew around, causing us to duck and cling to our partners, fearfully.

'Arawak Indian, period 600 to 1550.' The guide pointed to a sign. 'The Arawak Indians were the first inhabitants of the island. They died out when the Spanish came; worked to death, poor souls. They used to inhabit this cave.'

The spotlights cast shadows all around and the children cried, 'Suppose we meet up on duppies, Pastor? The Arawaks are all duppies now!'

The pastor said seriously, 'There are no spirits lingering here, children. The Arawaks are in heaven with our Father.'

'Runaway slaves used to hide in dis cave an' wait for de pirate ships to come in,' the guide said. 'Den they sailed away to freedom. But not all of dem escape. Some of dem still lingerin' in dis cave, deir spirits!'

There was fluttering overhead. Two blackbirds had found their way into the cave: they flew around in confusion.

The pastor said, 'Birds in the wilderness. Come along, children. We will not tarry here any longer.'

'Duppies, duppies,' the children wailed.

'There are no spirits in this cave,' Sister Myrtle said, 'I've been coming here since I was a girl and I can sense these things; there is nothing here, just mortals.'

'Nah.' The guide chuckled in a sinister manner, scaring us. 'Lost spirits. Guardians of de cave.'

The pastor said seriously: 'Let us say the Lord's Prayer: "Our Father in heaven, hallowed be thy name . . ." If there be unclean spirits present, Lord, cleanse them and set them free.'

The guide was already on his way, beckoning us. He said, 'It would tek more dan one "Our Father" to

31

release hundreds of trapped souls who sought sanctuary 'ere. Dis is a memorial to Arawaks an' Africans; no evil 'ere, jus' wronged spirits!'

A group of American and Chinese tourists caught up with us, huffing, puffing and bathed in perspiration. Meantime we were overcome with fear. The tourists rushed headlong towards the lake, fascinated by the history of the cave. Somewhere in the distance there was an opening. We saw a ray of sunlight.

'In the midst of darkness there is light,' Sister Martha said. 'Lead us out of the wilderness, guide.'

Felix and I had been holding hands tightly. Our palms were damp. There was green vegetation ahead and the cool breeze wafted into the cave, calming our racing hearts.

'There they go.' The pastor pointed after the birds. 'Look, children. The birds strayed into the cave by mistake.'

'Dat may be so.' The guide tossed back his dreadlocks proudly. 'But dat dohn explain why dose two blackbuds always stray eena de cave wheneber a party of schoolchildren appear. Is de ancestors, a tell yuh; dem want yuh all fe remember dem!'

The guide was the light of our world. He opened our eyes in the darkness, kept the memory of Africans and Arawaks alive. There was a heaviness in the cave. It was as if there were hundreds of eyes watching us, coveting our freedom.

'This place is haunted, Felix,' I said. 'It's as if there are hundreds of eyes watching us.'

'I know,' Felix said. 'I can sense it, too.'

Felix and I walked on and the guide said we looked like little soldiers marching through the valley of the shadow of death. All we needed were our banners proclaiming 'Freedom'. We marched ahead of the others, desperate to see the outside world, putting distance between us and the place where so many trapped spirits seemed to linger. When we were nearing the mouth of the cave, I stopped and stared at the jagged rocks, saying: 'I never want to see this cave again, Felix; it's trapped in the past.'

Felix said: 'Just think, Festus, we can never recapture today, not ever. Some day it will seem like a dream to us.'

'I wish we could be children for ever,' I said.

'Me too,' Felix said. 'I never want to grow up. I can't imagine us as grown men, going separate ways.'

The pastor overheard us. He said, 'Boys, when you are grown men, you will long to be children again. Leave the future alone and enjoy your childhood while you can.'

Felix turned to me and said, 'I've got a nail in my pocket, Festus. Let's write our names on this rock.'

The pastor and the others headed towards a bar at the mouth of the cave, where the Rastafarian guide was already preparing lime cordial with crushed ice for everyone.

Felix could think of nothing to write; he gave me the nail. I pondered. Then I wrote: 'Festus and Felix, Friends for Life; February 1965'. Our friendship had been declared to the world now. We walked into the daylight, confident that we would remain friends for ever.

4

One People

Felix and I rarely quarrelled but we found ourselves
squabbling about who really owned Jamaica. Having
visited Green Grotto Lake and seen the plaque
commemorating the Arawak Indians, I was adamant
that Jamaica belonged to the Arawaks first, the
Spanish next, then the British, followed by the
Africans. Felix was adamant that his people also
belonged in Jamaica. Of course, I was wrong but it
took a long time for me to realise it. We were on the
north coast of the island, and Aunt Hetty had said
that, after abolition, many ex-slaves migrated inland,
settling in our village. And when the Asians came,
they wandered the countryside, looking for work
once indentureship was up; some settled in our
village. Hence many of the villagers were of mixed
race.

Felix and I loved visiting the elderly parishioners.
They, like Aunt Hetty, were the last of the old breed
and some had no living relations: they were all born
in the latter part of the nineteenth century and they
knew real history. They were lonely individuals and
we did odd jobs for them, for which they gave us
money, mainly worthless farthings and pennies.

Felix and I had a rota: first we visited Father's
uncle, whom we called Great-Uncle Lance. He sat in
a chair on his verandah with a striped blanket
covering his knees. He trembled always. We thought
he was cold, and would wrap the blanket around his
shoulders. His verandah looked out on to a flower

34

garden where the grasshoppers hopped from the roses on to his lap; it was our job to chase them away.

Felix was afraid of Great-Uncle Lance, who was long and bony. His skin was wrinkled and his teeth were blackened. He had travelled in his youth and claimed to have fought in the Great War; he was said to be shell-shocked. He talked to the invisible friends of his youth, mumbling: 'Boysie, Jerel, lawd a macy! De bom' dem a com' dung: boom, boom, boom . . .'

'Howdy-do, Uncle Lance,' we said.

'Yuh late, bwoys.' He nodded. 'Mus' be lunchtime now.'

Father usually brought up breakfast of mint tea, boiled egg and porridge. He washed and changed Great-Uncle Lance and settled him on the verandah. Mother or Uncle Caesar's wife, Aunt Esther, visited at noon. Uncle Caesar came later, putting Great-Uncle Lance to bed.

It was mid-morning and Great-Uncle Lance was tired of sitting upright. He said, 'Bwoys, gimme a 'and. De body tired, sah: me pas' t'ree score 'ears an' ten long time now.'

We stood on either side of him and lifted him from the high-backed chair, helping him into a comfortable armchair. He smelled of carbolic soap and mint. He had a thermos of mint tea by his side which Mother had provided.

Great-Uncle Lance kept a jar of coins on his bedside table; he got a pension because he was a war veteran. He said, 'Festus, pass me dat jar.' He gave us four farthings to be shared between us. We took the coins reluctantly. He said: 'Bwoys, is wat dem teachin' oono a school? Four farthings mek a penny, yuh know.'

Our next visit was to an old lady called Aunt Vanda. She was dark-skinned and read the Bible constantly. Her cottage had been built soon after emancipation. It was surrounded by cedar trees and tangerine trees; a twisted path led up to the door.

Aunt Vanda had short grey hair. Her fingers were long and skinny and her long nails resembled claws. She also wore ill-fitting men's shoes: her husband had died long ago and she wore his shoes and socks. Whenever we visited Aunt Vanda, we sat on the grass outside her run-down cottage, waiting for the rooks to come home to their nest in a hole in the roof. Then we chased them away. Aunt Vanda joined in, too, running round and shooing the rooks. Afterwards we sat on the grass eating tangerines while the rooks sneaked into the nest. Aunt Vanda would take to her rocking-chair at the cottage door, rocking like a rag-doll and muttering, 'De likkle scamps.'

One day I said, 'Aunt Vanda, why do you chase the rooks away? I'm sure you like it when they sneak into the nest.'

She stopped rocking. 'Ah' me bwoy. Chasing de birds is me only pleasure in life, 'cept fe readin' de Bible.' She reached into her blouse, untying her thread-bag from her brassière strap. 'A penny fe yuh troubles, bwoys.' We left her rocking faster and faster.

We visited Uncle Hyman next. He lived in a large old house with very little furniture; he'd sold most of it to make ends meet. He had an old-fashioned radiogram and was always trying to tune into Cuba where he'd worked on a sugar estate in the 1920s, but he was deported with many others during the Great Depression. He loved Spanish music. His skin was white and scaly with patches of brown pigment on his face.

One day I said: 'Uncle Hyman, why is your skin white and brown, and why are your eyes green?'

We were sitting on the bank of the river. He said,

'Me puppa's peeple com' from Scotland, bwoys. 'Im married a negya ooman, but me tek afta 'is side o' de fambily. Is only the patchy-patchy face gimme weh.'

'I'm all mixed up, too,' Felix said.

'Mm.' Uncle Hyman looked into the water as the fishing-rod began to jerk. He raised the line and there was a fish wriggling in the air. He said: 'A know how yuh feel right now, frien'. Fish outa wata, like me.'

Felix and I stared at the struggling fish. It was our job to supply Uncle Hyman's bait. We gave him a jar of worms and he gave us a rusty penny to be shared between us. Then he threw the fish back into the river.

'Why did you do that?' I asked.

'De fish keep me company.' He smiled. 'Good day, bwoys.'

Our next stop took us to Aunt Beatrice's cottage. She was small and meagre. Her wrinkled skin seemed yellow and she had lots of liver spots. It was our job to polish the cottage floor with beeswax and then we shone it with brushes, which were made from coconut palms, until we saw our faces.

'Bwoys,' Aunt Beatrice said, 'a want dis floor fe shine like a dolla' piece.'

Aunt Beatrice had a fish-pond in her garden where she kept broad lilies and there were lots of marigolds in the yard. She gave us bread and honey, followed by goat's milk, once we'd finished our work. We hated the sickly sweet milk, but Aunt Beatrice said: 'Bwoys, drink yuh milk an' yuh will see wat sturdy bwoys yuh will be, 'specially yuh, Felix!'

Felix said: 'Aunt Beatrice, why is your skin yellow and why have you got Chinese eyes?'

'Me puppa's people came from China,' she said. 'Dem call me Chinaman pickney.'

'Just like Papa's people,' Felix said. 'Would you like to live in China?'

'Noh, sah,' she said. 'Dis is de promised land.'

'I thought Jamaica was the land of wood and water!' I exclaimed. 'Canaan is supposed to be the promised land.'

'Festus,' she said, 'drink yuh milk an' nyam yuh bread an' honey an' preten' yuh livin' eena paradise. Dat is de only way to get thru dis life.' She sighed. 'Where 'as yout' gone? In my day I was a belle.' She went into the cottage and returned with a small looking-glass. She gave us a sixpence each and stared at her reflection: 'Mirror, mirror, on de wall . . .'

'She lives in fairy-tale land, Felix,' I whispered.

We waved goodbye to Aunt Beatrice. Then Felix said, 'For a moment I thought she meant a real bell, Festus.'

'Same here,' I said, imagining Aunt Beatrice as the wicked witch in the story of Sleeping Beauty.

We called on Aunt Agatha next. She was an albino and she was very fat. There were breadfruit trees in the yard. She was always eating roasted or boiled breadfruits; it was our job to feed the leftovers to the pig. Aunt Agatha always had a kerosine pan of hog food on the boil, ready to feed the pigs.

We poured the swill into a long trough in the sty. Then, once the pigs finished eating, they sat at the far end of the sty, flapping their ears and grunting contentedly as we cleaned out the sty. Aunt Agatha stood at the opposite end, snorting, 'Get movin', yuh greedy pigs!'

No sooner had we finished cleaning out the sty than the pigs began to chase us around. They never bit us, but their slimy snouts touched our legs. They rushed around, grunting and squealing, providing entertainment for Aunt Agatha who was a widow. She snorted, 'Dat's it, me pets. Let dem wo'k fe dem money.' She gave us a farthing afterwards.

'Good day, Aunt Agatha,' I said. She did not reply because she was greedily eating a ripe banana. I turned to Felix and whispered, 'She reminds me of her pigs.'

'I know,' Felix said.

Our last stop took us to Aunt Kizzy's house. She was Father's kin. She was tall and thin with goofy teeth and big ears. She had a vegetable patch in which she grew carrots. She gave us carrot juice. Once we'd drunk the juice, we were expected to feed her rabbits and clean out the hutch.

'Festus, Felix,' Aunt Kizzy said. 'Dohn temp' me rabbits, bwoys; feed dem!'

Felix and I stood, facing the mesh-fronted hutch, tempting the rabbits with carrots. As soon as Aunt Kizzy appeared, we began to fuss over the rabbits. Then we cleaned out the hutch. The rabbits were very shrewd because they sat still until the hutch was cleaned out. But when it was time to put them back, they hopped around the vegetable patch, chasing us.

'Good bunnies.' Aunt Kizzy rocked on her heels, laughing and clapping. We coaxed the rabbits back into the hutch and Aunt Kizzy said, 'Bwoys, don't mind yuh maddy-maddy aunt. A need a bit of 'citement now an' den.' She reached into her apron pocket and fished out a sixpence.

Aunt Kizzy was crunching on a carrot and I whispered, 'Felix, she's crunching the carrot like a rabbit.'

'With those goofy teeth and big ears,' Felix muttered, 'she reminds me of a rabbit.'

'Com' again, bwoys.' Aunt Kizzy bit into the carrot.

Felix and I did not realise how important our village was, and all the people who lived in it, not until we'd read the motto on the Jamaica coat of arms: 'Out of Many, One People'. We began then to appreciate the contribution our people had made to the history of Jamaica.

5

The Cricket Match

Felix and I attended a school where the age range was from seven to sixteen-year-olds. The headmaster, Mr Lloyd, was a dark-skinned man who always wore short-sleeved plaid shirts, olive-coloured Terylene trousers and a matching tie, even on a hot day. He was of medium height and going bald. There was a fountain pen sticking out of his shirt pocket and a white handkerchief, with which he used to dab his forehead. He was born in Cuba in the year of the Great War – 1914. His parents had gone there seeking work but, like Uncle Hyman, they were deported, back to Jamaica during the Great Depression. He spoke fluent Spanish and liked to dismiss a child in the schoolyard, saying, '*Vamoose!*' Or he would wave a favourite pupil off. '*Adiós, amigo.*'

All the children dreaded being singled out by Mr Lloyd, whose highly polished brown shoes squeaked all the time. He would enter the classroom and say: 'You, boy! Where is the equator? What is the square root of sixteen? How do you spell Mississippi and how do we get rainfall? Speak up!'

Felix was singled out and he was so nervous, he forgot that Japan was the land of the rising sun, and Norway the land of the midnight sun. Mr Lloyd snapped: 'Stretch forth thy right hand, boy. There is no room in this school for dunces!' He was flexing a cane. He brought it down on Felix's palm.

At break Felix wept. I said, 'Never mind. Everyone

knows you're not a dunce. Mr Lloyd is really strict; he even frightens the younger teachers.'

There were two schools in our district, Norman Manley House and Bustamante House, for all the children from the surrounding villages as well as ours. Our school was Norman Manley House. It was perched on a hill. It had a slate-tiled roof, unlike the other school near by which had a corrugated roof that leaked whenever it rained. There were almond trees in our schoolyard and bamboo trees on the hillside. The bamboos made good wickets as well as the canes with which Mr Lloyd chastised offenders.

There was tough competition between the two schools: occasionally fights broke out in the evenings when the children from both schools crossed paths. They were always hurling insults at each other, each insisting their school produced the cleverest pupils and the best cricketers. But no one knew for certain because both schools were competitive and could boast that several of their pupils had won scholarships to secondary school.

Cricket was a game that was played with enthusiasm at our school. Felix and I had just celebrated our tenth birthdays when the annual cricket match was held between the two schools. Everyone was invited, provided they brought along their own food and drink.

Mr Lloyd opened the match, saying: 'Cricket is the national sport of the British Caribbean, boys. Play fair and remember to be good sports: no cheating or squabbling.'

To be in the schoolyard when a cricket match was in progress was something not to be missed, if you were a cricket fan. Even if you'd left school, you were welcomed back, still a part of the team. Barnaby, Osman and lots of other young men turned up to play cricket or cheer. Occasionally a fathers' match was organised by Mr Lloyd on a Sunday afternoon. Children stood in amazement looking at their strict fathers running up and down the pitch, shouting like children: 'Lbw, bowl 'im out! Knock 'im fe six, man . . .'

Mr Lloyd often told us the history of cricket: how the colonials played cricket with the workers on the sugar estates, and how in 1900 the first West Indian touring party visited England and several black players were included. Cricket went beyond the boundaries of race and class. Men like Learie Constantine of Trinidad, Gary Sobers of Barbados and our own George Headley were black cricketers to be proud of. They were so good they'd played in Europe.

Felix was a fast bowler. He was always in demand to play for our school. But I secretly disliked the game. I was good at keeping my wickets standing, but not particularly good at hitting the ball. The only time I was bullied at school was when I played cricket. I could never hit the ball properly. Try as I might, I just wasn't cut out for the game. The new cedar bats that Osman had made for Felix and me aroused envy in the other boys, but I would have preferred something else: my bat drew attention to me; I hated it really.

Felix took his cricket seriously and, sometimes when he was playing, he played with all his might, forgetting about me. It was all right for him: he excelled himself on the field. But I was always dropping a catch. Then the boys would get cross and snap, 'You're so clumsy, Festus. Why can't you be like Felix? He's really good!'

Afterwards Felix would tell me not to worry. It was only a game, nothing more. But I did worry, I was letting the side down. Whenever there was a big match, I simply refused to play. I didn't want to take the blame if we lost. Besides, I hated competitions; I

43

only ever wanted to compete with myself.

'We'd be better off getting one of the girls to play instead of Festus,' the boys would snap. 'He's useless!'

'Felix, Felix,' the chant went up. 'We want Felix . . .'

How I hated it when they called for Felix. Today was no exception. The match was between the two schools and we were one player short; I couldn't refuse to play. Father, Mas Rupee, Barnaby and Osman were there, too. A coin was tossed: heads, our team was first to play, and each boy was quickly dismissed. Then came my turn to bat and I was instantly charged with lbw. Father and Barnaby witnessed my disgrace. And to top it all, some of our best players were absent, suffering from chicken-pox.

'He's out already,' someone shouted. 'Let's slight him!'

No one would speak to me. I felt really miserable. I dropped my bat and rushed towards Father, weeping. 'It wasn't my fault. I didn't expect the ball to come flying at me so fast. I thought it was going to hit me on the shin!'

'Never mind, son,' Father said. 'I was never any good at cricket, always dropping the catch and getting bowled out.'

'You didn't try hard enough, Festus.' Osman frowned.

'Our school is going to lose the trophy because of me,' I cried. 'It's all my fault. I hate cricket.'

'You can't win them all, Festus,' Father said. 'Leave it to Felix, son. He'll save the day.'

But Felix couldn't save the day: he was not as good a batsman as he was a fast bowler. We shouldn't have gone in first. He never got a chance to bowl out our rivals. One by one our players were bowled out and not even the chanting of: 'Norman Manley's boys dem a warriors, Norman Manley's boys dem a warriors . . . Anywhere you go, you hear dem say, Norman Manley's boys dem a warriors . . .' could deter our rivals.

'Bustamante's boys dem a warriors, Bustamante's boys dem a warriors. Anywhere you go, you hear dem say, Bustamante's boys dem a warriors . . .' the rivals sang.

The teachers also encouraged the rivalry. They stood on opposite sides of the field, cheering their schools on.

'Come on, Norman Manley House . . .'

'Come on, Bustamante House . . .' came the reply.

When you got close to the teachers you could see the look of determination on their faces; there was no room for losers. The battle raged on and on because there was a sports trophy to be collected by the winning team. The headmaster of the defeated school had to present the trophy, and so each headmaster had a good reason for wanting his school to win.

The headmaster of Bustamante House was a tall man called Mr Llewelyn. He was very proud and hated defeat. There was rivalry between the two headmasters; they always kept straight faces during a match. But today Mr Llewelyn was smiling.

'It's all your fault, Festus,' the boys said afterwards. 'You couldn't even hit the ball. You lost us the trophy.'

'Take no notice of them,' Felix said. 'It just wasn't our day. Anyway, we'll win the trophy next time.'

Mr Lloyd presented Mr Llewelyn with the trophy. 'Chicken-pox kept my best players away today, Llewelyn. And it's a pity our team went in first. Felix, our fast bowler, would have certainly bowled your boys out, had they played first.'

Mr Llewelyn held the trophy, saying: 'I seem to

remember you telling me last year to accept defeat gracefully, Lloyd!'

'Hm.' Mr Lloyd gave a wide smile.

'See, Festus.' Felix handed me my bat. 'It wasn't your fault. Next time we'll thrash them.'

'Not me.' I refused to be comforted.

Felix said, 'You just feel shamed, that's all. Once you've mastered the game, you'll be all right; I promise you. We'll practise later on.'

'Felix,' I said, 'I can't stand cricket. I know you like it, but I hate it.'

'Listen to you,' he said. 'One day you'll be cheering the West Indies on; mark my words.'

'I doubt it,' I said. 'Cricket is not my game.'

Felix gave up. He realised that there was no point in trying to persuade me further. Somehow he sensed that I would never share his enthusiasm, for I couldn't get over the shame of being bowled out on the first ball.

6

Dancing Shoes

Felix and I walked barefoot during the week, and on Sundays we wore shoes to church, though some of the children wore shoes all the time. We envied the boys in their shiny pointed-toed, leather shoes which their relatives had sent from abroad. But our parents couldn't afford to keep us in everyday shoes. We longed for the day when we could buy our own shoes with the money we had saved from doing odd jobs for the elders in the village. But farthings were worthless and pennies took a long time to grow: we needed ten shillings each and we could not meet the target.

On a Saturday afternoon I went down to Felix's house. Missis Leena had become a full-time seamstress since Matilda's wedding and everyone had praised the beautiful wedding dress. The only problem was that people never had the money to pay for Missis Leena's labour. She was always out of pocket. Right now she'd just finished making a red gingham dress. She had an old-fashioned iron with a spout. She filled it up with coal and stood on the verandah ironing the dress.

Matilda sat in a beaten-up wicker chair, watching Missis Leena as she worked. She was plaiting her thick black hair. She said, 'Mother, charity begins at home.'

Missis Leena said, 'When yuh give yuh also get your share, Matty. Dohn worry, sooner or later me clients will pay up.'

47

'Matty is right,' Felix mumbled.

'Felix, is wat yuh grumblin' 'bout now?' Missis Leena splashed some water on the face of the iron, testing it.

Felix and I sat on the verandah counting our money, which we kept in a large match box. We had stopped doing odd jobs for the elderly villagers because we were bone tired and our farthings and pennies were taking a long time to mount up. There had to be another way to earn money quickly.

'We will be old men before we get those shoes.' Felix stopped counting. 'We'll never be able to afford those black, shiny, leather shoes. It's not fair.'

'Festus, Felix.' Missis Leena laboured over the ironing board. 'If nature 'ad intended fe us to wear shoes, we would neber 'ave been given toes. Look at my toes: dem full of corn and bunions 'cause of those pointed-toe, spike-heel shoes.'

Felix and I giggled. Missis Leena was plagued with bunions, yet she wouldn't part with her fashionable shoes, which sank into the linoleum on the floor or the grass in the churchyard. Most of the women suffered a similar fate, though Mother and Matilda never did. They always wore flat, black lace-up shoes or sandals.

'Festus, Felix.' Missis Leena put down the iron. 'A thin face with a mouth full of teeth, including two gold canines, frowned at us. Her long black hair was plaited down her back. 'A don't like red-yeye pickneys.'

'You're right, Mother,' Matilda agreed.

Felix and I stared at the match box in silence. We were shamefaced because we'd been brought up to forsake envy, yet we found ourselves envying the children in their fancy shoes.

'Can Felix come down to my house, Missis Leena?' I asked. 'I've got a great idea.'

Missis Leena nodded. She switched on the radio, smiling. 'We jus' in time fe 'ear *Dulcimena: Her Life in Town*, Matty.' (This was a daily radio story about a country girl who had gone to Kingston to work.) 'Poor Dulcimena.' Missis Leena shook her head. 'De trials an' tribulations dat poor girl haffe suffer, servantin' fe dose high-class peeple.'

We left Missis Leena and Matilda listening to *Dulcimena*, shaking their heads sadly. We went to see my father. One of the hens on the farm had had twelve chicks: they were black, brown and yellow. Father was counting them. He was such a big man, he looked really clumsy as he held the two black chicks.

'Can we have two of the chicks, Father?' I asked.

Father must have been in a good mood because he said without hesitating, 'All right, but only if you're prepared to look after them yourselves. I don't have time to chase hawks and mongooses.'

Felix kept looking at my father who was cooing at the chicks. He whispered, 'Your father's gone cuckoo, Festus.'

Father gave us two yellow chicks and it was our job to protect them from the hawks and mongooses that roamed the farm. We took our job seriously and we stopped going to Sunday-school so we could watch the chicks. Anyway, we hated going because the children were always showing off in their new shoes.

The chicks were growing up fast. At three months old they were really big. There was a commotion in the yard one day. The hens spotted a mongoose and the brood scattered when the hens began to peck the mongoose. Meantime a hawk appeared and snatched a yellow chick. It flew off and sat in a tree on the hillside with the chick in its mouth. The mongoose stole a black chick and got away too. Felix and I began to weep.

Mother came out from the kitchen. Her eyes were streaming for she'd been peeling onions to make pepper-pot soup. She said, 'Boys, dry your eyes. Hawks and mongooses always take chickens. It's nature's way.'

'Nature is very cruel.' Felix puffed out his bottom lip.

'Boys,' Mother said, 'the little song says: "Chicken merry, hawk deh near an' when 'im deh near, yuh mus' beware"; so simmer dung.' She left us then.

'There's a song for everything in Jamaica!' Felix snapped.

That Sunday we went to church. We had not been for a few weeks. The church was painted white and the sun had scorched the peeling paintwork. There were vines growing up the walls where a crack or two had appeared. The pews had worn badly with age and the chipped wood pinched our thighs: Felix and I wore short trousers while most of the boys wore long pants.

The pastor enjoyed preaching the gospel, and the service went on for an eternity. Aunt Hetty would rap her walking-stick on the floor impatiently whenever the pastor prolonged the service. Today he stretched out his arms on the pulpit. 'Brothers and sisters, God will not let us thirst in the wilderness for much longer. He will answer our prayers.'

All of a sudden the adults were talking about the island-wide drought. Many animals had died of thirst and huge tankers came round regularly, carrying gallons of water. Women and children queued up in the village square with their aluminium buckets and butter-pans, waiting their turn to get water; the river had turned to mud and a few of the catchment tanks were almost dry. Felix and I never took the drought seriously because our parents had catchment tanks; we had enough water, though we used it sparingly. The congregation sang, 'Send down the rain, send down the rain, send down the gospel rain . . .'

'Alleluia! Praise the Lord!' The congregation rocked, strong in their faith. On this occasion Aunt Hetty was absent. She was suffering from dengue fever and was confined to bed.

Felix and I stared out the window, expecting to see rain. The people sang so heartily that we thought the Lord would open the windows of heaven. No rain came and we wondered if our village had been forgotten by God. We hadn't even noticed that the crops were blighted and food was scarce until our parents began to complain. We were so wrapped up in our desire to own those coveted dancing shoes, everything else took second place.

After preaching and beseeching the Lord to feed His children, the pastor led the choir into singing 'Guide me, O Thou great Jehovah, pilgrim through this barren land . . .'

There was a feeling of solidarity. People lifted their hands to heaven and rocked on their heels, causing the floorboards to creak.

The service ended and Felix and I were the first to leave, eager to avoid the other children, especially since many of the boys hadn't forgotten the cricket match.

Back at my house Felix and I sat in a grapefruit tree, eating the sweet grapefruits. The chicks were scratching under the tree and I said, 'Felix, it's time to sell them.'

'We can't, Festus,' Felix wailed. 'Those are our pets.'

'I know,' I said. 'But we have no choice.'

'You're right,' Felix said. 'We have no choice.'

It was customary for Mother to go to market at St Ann's Bay on Saturdays to buy the weekly shopping. The very next Saturday morning Felix and I asked her to sell the chicks for us and use the money from the sale to buy our shoes. She agreed because she said we had behaved in a responsible manner. We were really excited, especially when Father measured our feet on brown paper and cut out the shapes.

In the afternoon the country bus sounded from afar and we rushed down to the crossroads to meet Mother. The bus was crowded with shoppers and higglers, returning with their bankras loaded with food and other wares.

'But, but . . .' I stammered when the chicks jumped out of Mother's bankra at the crossroads. 'What about our shoes?'

'I don't believe it!' Felix exclaimed. 'No shoes?'

The passengers laughed and winked at us, as if they knew something we didn't. The conductor was called Kambah. He had a patch over one eye. He shouted: 'Gwane, driver. Gwane, man!'

The bus moved off and we went home to lunch: calloo 'n' saltfish with boiled green bananas which Granny Una had prepared. But we were filled with disappointment. We couldn't eat a thing. We sat there mashing our bananas with our forks.

'Festus, Felix, go and wash your feet,' Father said.

Well, we almost tripped over Buster, the dog, as we raced towards the aluminium bath pan in the backyard, washed and rushed back.

'I believe you boys have been hankering after these.' Mother handed us each a pair of patent shoes.

We slipped our feet into the shoes and stood on the verandah, dancing. 'Ska, ska, ska, Jamaican ska . . .'

Sunday morning bright and early Felix and his parents stopped at our gate, on their way to church.

Missis Leena's mouth seemed exceptionally crowded with teeth as she grinned at us. Mas Rupee's arms were far too long for his white shirt.

'Bwoys, yuh better dan me.' Mas Rupee stared at our feet. 'A neber wear shoes till a tu'n twenty-one.'

'Rupee, time changin',' Missis Leena said.

Mas Rupee said: 'When me was a bwoy, me used to run around wid de seat of me homemade calico shorts worn out. Nowadays bwoys only want fe wear ready-made long pants.'

'The good old days,' Mother said.

'Noh sah,' Granny Una said. 'De nineteen-thirties woz turbulent 'ears: de Great Depression, strikes, riots; the bad old days.'

We set off for church. Our village was still suffering from the drought. The grass looked as if it had been scorched and many plants were blighted. The beautiful countryside now reminded me of a wilted flower garden.

During the service, the pastor preached and preached. 'Brothers and sisters, have faith; it can move mountains.'

But the parishioners had lost faith and not even a rousing chorus of 'Send down the rain, send down the rain, send down the gospel rain . . .' could revive them.

'Alleluia!' Granny Una said. 'Praise the Lord.'

The pastor opened his arms. 'Must Jesus bear the cross alone and all the world go free?'

'No, there's a cross for everyone,' the elders chanted.

But it was not easy, rousing the spirits of people who had prayed in vain for rain. The choir sang, 'Softly and tenderly Jesus is calling, calling for you and for me . . .'

The congregation offered up more prayers. The

service ended and the adults greeted friends, relatives, neighbours. Meantime the children congregated behind the church, dancing.

'They're not dancing the ska!' I cried out in frustration.

'Where have you two been hiding?' they asked. 'Don't you ever listen to the radio? We're dancing the rock-steady.'

Bap! The ska had gone out of fashion, just like that. The rock-steady had taken its place. Felix and I felt like crying. But the children pulled us into the circle they'd formed, and reluctantly we found ourselves practising the rock-steady to the chimes of the church bell.

7

Election Fever

Uncle Caesar, Father's brother, was a popular figure in the district because he owned the only grocery shop in our community. It was situated in the village square. The sqaure itself served as a meeting place for the villagers, especially the farmers and unemployed men who sat on the shop piazza, listening to the radio. Often they turned up the volume of the radio and sang aloud, singing the latest jamma.

There were several shops in the village square: the grocery shop, the rum bar, the tailor's shop, the post office and the shoemaker's shop. These shops carried the life of the community; there was always a lot of noise, made worse by the screeching of tyres on gravel at noon when the red Royal Mail van arrived. There was laughter and squabbles outside the post office where women and children queued up to receive letters and parcels from abroad, saying to the plump, fair-skinned post mistress (whose light-brown hair was worn in a bun), 'Good day, PM. Any letters today?' Meantime the men in the rum bar knocked dominoes on wood, discussing the state of our nation.

It was 1967 and radios carried news of election fever in Kingston. The villagers spent a great deal of time gaping at the huge cars which rolled by, slowing down so that we could all get a glimpse of the important-looking faces staring into space. The chauffeurs of these well-dressed individuals would occasionally stop and ask directions, causing the men in the rum bar to reel out, saying: ''Old on, driver.

Me know de way to Kingston . . . You cahn go wrong; just keep on de straight an' narrow, man.'

On this occasion, one of the farmers said, 'Hush up, man. Is w'en since yuh know Town? Mek me direct yuh noh, sah!'

Long after the car had disappeared the men stared into the distance, saying, 'Wonder which politician dat? 'Im nearly white, must be Syrian or Lebanese. Wat a way 'im cream suit stoshus! We put dese high-class peeple up dere eena gover'ment 'ouse, an' all of a sudden dem forget is who did vote fe dem!'

'Wonder if that was Bustamante?' Felix said.

'No,' I said. 'He's retired, probably Norman Manley.'

Felix recited: 'Lawyer, doctor, Syrian, chief . . .'

It was a childhood saying, meaning, 'What will you be when you grow up?' Many children wanted to be a Syrian because the Syrians were the chief businessmen and politicians in Jamaica.

'Chief,' I said. 'I want to be an Indian chief.'

The car had woken up a lot of dust in the square because the road was unpaved; it settled on everything. We felt embarrassed for our people because the politicians rarely got out of the cars. It was as if they were afraid that the dust and the farmers, in their sweat-stained clothes and mud-caked water-boots, would soil their stylish-looking suits.

This election was a special occasion because it was announced that the MP for our parish would be passing through, canvassing. The villagers intended to ask him when we'd be getting a new road. The village square overflowed with people bickering about which party was best: Norman Manley's People's National Party or Alexander Bustamante's Jamaica Labour Party?

Sister Martha, the Sunday-school teacher, had decided that the twins, Marigold and Primrose, should present the MP with two bouquets. They strolled around the square rehearsing their speech: 'Distinguished guest . . . on behalf of the people of this district, we now present you with these flowers . . .'

Dusk came, the flowers wilted, the twins shed hot tears and their parents took them home, complaining, 'Last time dese pickneys gwine tu'n flower-girls fe anybody!'

'Why yuh peeple won't tek heed?' one of the farmers said. 'Politicians too high-up fe shake 'ands wid country peeple. Dem only use sweet-mouth ober de radio fe catch us.'

My parents and Felix's parents stood outside Uncle Caesar's shop, drinking Dragon Stout.

'Whoop, bam, pardon me.' Missis Leena belched. 'Word is jus' wind.'

The crowd broke up and people strolled home with their shoulders hunched up, cursing their MP who had caused them to behave like children waiting to see Santa Claus.

Uncle Caesar's wife was called Aunt Esther. She was a small woman with greying hair. She wore two thick silver bangles and she kept saying: 'Shop close, shop close; time to go home . . .'

Felix and I were fascinated by Aunt Esther's eyes. They were light-brown with specks of yellow, resembling gold dust. She locked up the shop while Uncle Caesar went off to the back room where he poured kerosine oil into bottles. She said, 'Boys, the tourist season is about to begin and I don't want you staring at those glassy-eyed Americans. It is bad manners to stare at strangers.'

'We just like to look at their eyes,' we said. 'They're so glassy, just like cats' eyes.'

Mother went off to Aunt Esther's kitchen to make cocoa tea for everyone. Father and Mas Rupee sat in a corner discussing the day's event. The low ceiling with its exposed wooden beams seemed to be pressing down on us as Mas Rupee said: 'Yuh wrong, yuh know, Missis Esther. Politicians suppose fe walk 'bout an' shake de 'ands dat cast de vote fe dem.'

'Crackers and cocoa tea.' Mother came in with a tray. 'Why waste breath on people who don't even know we exist?'

'Yuh rite, Lois.' Missis Leena nodded.

Uncle Caesar was a big man who reeked of kerosine oil. He supplied the oil which the villagers burned in their lamps. He came into the shop, saying: 'Salvan, it's your turn to look after Uncle Lance. I pray the Lord will soon take him. The poor man is worn out with all that mumbling. This morning he said: "Chi-bum, chi-bum . . . I'm a scientist".'

Felix and I smiled; Great-Uncle Lance had a new saying.

'Don't remind me,' Father sighed. 'Lois and I are worn out: we called on Aunt Hetty earlier on. She had a metal drum in the yard and it was full of stagnant water, harbouring mosquitoes. We got rid of the water and the drum. Then we cleaned the house and lit a coal stove on the verandah, working up a smoke, to get rid of the mosquitoes. The wretched things bit her all over, gave her dengue fever. We are worn out after all that work. Can you deal with Uncle Lance tonight?'

'All right,' Uncle Caesar said. 'Your turn tomorrow.'

The adults dunked crackers into their cocoa tea, fretting about Great-Uncle Lance. They shook their heads. 'Once a man, twice a child.' Great-Uncle Lance needed constant attention.

We finished our late supper, eager to get home to Granny Una. She'd stayed away as she had no faith in politicians. Then we left Uncle Caesar and Aunt

Esther. The village square was empty. My uncle's shop had lost the hustle and bustle of earlier on, and both he and my aunt seemed lonely as they stood on the shop piazza, waving. 'Walk good.'

The following evening Felix and I returned to Uncle Caesar's shop. Nowadays we followed him round the village as he went from house to house, collecting money which the villagers owed him. They often put their grocery bills on the slate till they could afford to pay. But sometimes those bills went unpaid for months. Then my uncle would take to his horse Fagan while Felix and I rode our fathers' donkeys.

Felix and I used to think going to church was a sure sign that the villagers were staunch Christians. How wrong we were.

First we visited Brother Daniel who had round cheeks and shifty eyes. His stout-looking wife Sister Loretta wore a white turban and thick-rimmed glasses.

'Good evening, Brother Caesar,' they said. 'And how is Festus and Felix today?'

'Fine thank you, mam, sir,' we replied.

Brother Daniel always complained about how badly his crops were doing. He insisted Uncle Caesar accepted ducks' eggs as payment. He placed them in a basket while the ducks surrounded us, quacking as if they wanted their eggs back. They calmed down once Felix stooped to quack with them. When we rode away from the cottage Brother Daniel's shifty eyes followed us. He and his wife claimed to have seen the light. Occasionally they preached in the village square, pleading with sinners to repent because the coming of the Lord was near. They walked around with two canes, flexing the things and hitting out, saying the Lord had instructed them to chastise sinners.

Next we called on Brother Simeon. He and his wife

Sister Gloria sat on the verandah reading the Bible or singing 'Onward, Christian Soldiers!' They said, 'Greetings, Brother Caesar. And how is Festus and Felix today?'

'Fine thank you, mam, sir,' we chanted.

'The Lord moves in a mysterious way,' they said. 'We were just talking about you, Brother Caesar. You're not called Caesar for nothing; you're a true emperor.'

My uncle had heard it all before. He showed his big white teeth. 'Render to Caesar the things that are Caesar's.'

Sister Gloria pursed her lips, narrowed her eyes and stared at Brother Simeon, who went to the back of the yard. He returned, tugging a squealing pig on a lead.

We set off with the pig struggling, the donkeys braying and Fagan blowing until we reached Brother Timothy and Sister Zara's place. Brother Timothy had a double chin and he played a concertina. His merino showed under his white shirt which was buttoned up to the neck. He wore brown-rimmed spectacles.

'Greetings,' he said. 'Brother Caesar, I've got nothing to offer you except a bunch of ripe bananas.'

Sister Zara wore a plaid dress and a turban. She was straight and bony. She had a sly look about her and she played the organ in church most Sundays; she played out of tune occasionally. She stared at the banana trees in the yard. 'Boys, I hope you're not training to be debt collectors?'

Felix and I were lost for words whenever we visited Sister Zara and her husband. They hated paying their bills and always tried to make my uncle feel mean for not being a cheerful giver. As we rode away from the cottage I said: 'Uncle Caesar, why do you let the people take goods on credit when you know they don't like paying up?'

'Boys,' he said, 'man traded by other means before money was invented. Besides, when I sell these goods at the market I get more money than was owing to me. Who is the wise one?'

Our next visit was to Brother Jeremy who was a thin man with a beard and watery dark eyes. His wife Sister Agnes was an obese woman who had been embroidering a white sheet for as long as we could recall.

'Greetings, folks,' they said. 'We were expecting you to pass this way today.' They produced a basket of ackees; the yellow vegetables with their red skin and black eyes seemed to be watching us.

Brother Jeremy said: 'Brother Caesar, have you ever heard the story of the needle and the camel?'

Felix and I had recited the verse over and over at Sunday-school. We thought my uncle had no chance of getting through the gates of heaven because the scripture says, 'It is easier for a camel to go through a needle's eye than for a rich man to enter into the kingdom of heaven.'

We set off once again, calling on Brother Zebedee who wore a tie and bicycle clips to keep his shirt sleeves up. His wife Sister Martha, the Sunday-school teacher, wore a starched white dress and a white turban.

'Good evening, folks,' they said. 'We were hoping you wouldn't turn up.' They stared at the swaying coconut trees in the yard. 'All we can offer you is a bunch of coconuts.'

Brother Zebedee wore a broad smile as he picked a whole bunch of coconuts from a dwarf-looking tree. Then he placed them in one of the hampers.

Sister Martha said, 'Boys, money is the root of all evil.'

Uncle Caesar smiled and we set off once more. He said, 'Boys, don't be fooled by a smiling face. Be careful of people who show their teeth too often and watch out for shifty eyes.'

That Sunday we went to church and the pastor preached and preached about raising money to repair the church. He said: 'Brothers and sisters, dig deep into your pockets. We need money to repair our chapel.' He took one of the collection plates round, saying: 'Render to Caesar the things that are Caesar's and to God the things that are God's!'

'Give generously, Caesar.' Aunt Esther nudged my uncle, who had dropped a shilling in the collection plate.

The pastor wore a broad smile when Uncle Caesar placed a five-pound note in the plate. He faced the congregation: 'God bless Brother Caesar. He's a good Christian.'

8

The Great House

York Castle was a plantation house on the outskirts of our village; it had a history of sugar and slavery. The villagers' ancestors had toiled for the backras on the property, either as field slaves or house slaves. Nowadays the property was owned by the bauxite company who used the land for cattle rearing. Once the cattle had matured, they were shipped off to America where they were slaughtered and the beef sold in supermarkets. In their place came the tourists, in the high season, riding around the countryside, looking down on the villagers.

There was an air of mystery surrounding York Castle. This was probably because the property was surrounded by stone walls and to enter the premises you had to climb the stone walls or enter through a huge iron gate. The gate was usually opened by the overseer, Busha, or the hired hands working on the property. Busha was a short brown-skinned man with curly hair. He drove a new, dark-green, Land Rover which was provided by the bauxite company who mined aluminium in the red earth of the countryside, though our village was spared the assault.

There was a sign at the gate of York Castle saying trespassers would be prosecuted. But they were never caught because the villagers were too proud to scale the walls in the daytime. At night they picked pimentos growing wild, oranges, grapefruits, jackfruits and breadfruits. In the distance the electric lights twinkled up at the great house which was set back from the road, elevated on its whitewashed foundation. The great house had numerous windows and wide steps leading up to a kind of balcony, not a verandah, where a mahogany door was visible. Peacocks strutted around the well-kept lawn, opening their wings and making mating sounds.

There was not a person in our village who hadn't secretly dreamed of owning York Castle. There was a television set which ran off a generator. It went 'Du-do, du-do, du-do . . .' Sound travelled in the night and you could hear the racket if you were standing in the village square. Very few of the villagers had seen the inside of York Castle, but they made up stories from the information they'd gathered from hired hands working on the property. It was said that the bathroom was tiled with marbles. Felix and I imagined hundreds of tiny marbles resembling cats' eyes, staring at the tourists who slipped about on the little objects. There was running water in the kitchen and bathroom, supplied by a huge catchment tank. We thought the great house was indeed heaven on earth. A person could die happily up there.

Another thing that fascinated us about York Castle was the fact that in the autumn the trees were naked and then the house was exposed and could be seen from the main road. We stood in awe, staring, dreaming. Also, since there were no tourists around we could stand for as a long as possible, with no one to glare at us. But in the summer the trees stretched forth their branches and the great house was shielded from prying eyes.

In the summer of 1967 the property was rented by a group of Americans. Felix and I were casually strolling along a dusty road when we met the tourists. We almost collided with them as we came round a bend in the road. Their horses reared and neighed and we stood back, trembling. The adults frowned, we'd frightened their horses, and the children hoisted themselves in their saddles, staring at us as if we were strange creatures. The horses pawed the gravel, no one spoke. We stood aside, feeling small compared with those straight-backed strangers sitting on those huge neighing beasts. The smell of dung came at us and we hated the tourists and the horses for making us feel inferior.

Another day Felix and I had been to Uncle Caesar's shop to buy cornmeal for Granny Una who was making corn pone. We were just about to leave when a party of Americans rode in. The women all had mean-looking red lips. The men wore denims and plaid shirts. There were several children present. Their horses kicked up dust in the square, neighing.

'Do they sell plum jam?' One of the women patted the mane of a black horse.

'Do they sell marmalade?' another asked. (They stared into the shop, but they weren't addressing my aunt and uncle.)

The men dismounted from the horses. They entered the shop and stared at the well-stocked shelves. There was a fridge in a dark corner, making a chugging noise as if going up a hill. It was operated on bottled gas. Meantime Aunt Esther cleaned the counter with an old rag.

'Do they sell ginger beer?' A lanky man with hair the colour of Aunt Kizzy's carrots stared at the shelves.

Aunt Esther put the rag under the counter. She opened the fridge and said, 'We've run out of ginger beer; will this do?'

'Well, would you look at that!' the man exclaimed. 'Pepsi Cola in the back of the beyond!'

Uncle Caesar coughed. 'We don't sell marmalade,

or plum jam but we sell guava jelly.' He took a jar off the shelf.

'How exotic!' The women exclaimed. 'Guava jelly . . .'

Uncle Caesar and Aunt Esther stood on the opposite side of the counter, looking really patient.

'Can you direct us to Edinburgh Castle?' someone said.

A few unemployed men were sitting on the shop piazza, playing dominoes and listening to the radio. One of them jumped up. 'Yeah, man. Me can direc' yuh. Jus' follow de straight road 'til yuh reach the nex' distric'.'

The tourists stood inside Uncle Caesar's shop drinking Pepsi. They declined the guava jelly, paid for their drink with dollars, mounted their horses and rode off, leaving a cloud of dust and the smell of horses' dung behind.

Uncle Caesar sighed. 'I wish those Americans would change their dollars into pound notes!'

One of the unemployed men banged a domino on the rickety table. 'Americans t'ink them own Jimaica. Dem spen' de dollas an' cents like wata flowin'. Anybody would tink money grow 'pon trees in 'Merica!'

Felix and I waited until the tourists were out of sight before we set off home.

Next day Missis Leena sent Felix and me on an errand up to the gate of York Castle. Her sister, Aunt Rachel, had got a job up at the great house, living in as a kind of housekeeper. She wasn't allowed visitors and she was sworn never to repeat what went on; she never did. Well, we never heard any of the stories.

Aunt Rachel was supposed to be preparing corn on the cob for the tourists, who were going to have a barbecue on the lawn, weather permitting. Missis

Leena had given Felix and me two bankras of sweet corn to take up to York Castle where Busha, the overseer, was expecting us. We stood at the gate, waiting. We couldn't see Busha and there was no bell on the gate. We climbed the stone wall and stood, shielding our eyes from the sun, observing the palm trees and the straight road which led up to the great house. Suddenly we sighted Busha's Land Rover coming down the path, followed by the sound of galloping on the main road. We felt really silly, standing on the wall, gaping.

'Caught you!' came an English voice. 'Trespassers! What shall we do with the little beggars?'

'We were only . . .' Our voices sounded really guilty.

'Is alright, baas.' Busha jumped out of the jeep on the opposite side of the wall. 'Is Miss Rachel's nephew an' 'im frien'. Dem bring som' corn fe lunch. Dem not trespassin'.'

'Look at those poor little boys,' said a child with an American accent. 'They've brought food for our lunch. Give them some money, Uncle.' He hoisted himself in the saddle.

The bearded Englishman fished into the pocket of his white baggy trousers which narrowed from the knees downward. 'Here you are, sonny boy.' He stared at Felix. 'Come and get it.'

Felix and I stood stock-still on the wall, feeling inferior. The thought hadn't crossed our minds that we could jump down. Why, oh why, did we have to climb that wall?

'Poor little things,' drawled one of the women. (They were the same people we'd seen in the village square.) 'I think they're afraid of us. Best to drop the money, Richard; they'll pick it up once we've gone.'

The man threw a few cents on the ground. The

coins rolled along, spun and fell flat. The party rode off, laughing. We climbed down frowning.

Busha whistled and two dogs jumped out of the open-topped Land Rover. He reached into his trouser pocket, took out a soiled, white handkerchief and wiped his perspiring face. 'Dese Americans t'ink all country peeple a poor things. Dem facety, sah.' He picked up the cents. 'Finders keepers.' He went through the gate, closed it and called out: 'Tyrone, Jerome, com' we go ketch trespassers, bwoys!'

Two large black dogs jumped up on the front seat, climbed over the back and sat in the Land Rover with their tongues hanging out. Then Busha drove off, tooting the horn.

Felix and I were vexed. First time we'd ever been called beggars, and we couldn't tell anyone; our parents would have been angry and the children at school would have laughed at us. They never stood by the gate of York Castle, for fear of being insulted by the tourists. But in our eagerness to see the great house, we had forgotten how rude the tourists could be.

'I feel so 'shamed.' Felix pursed his lips.

'I know.' I cocked my right ear. All of a sudden there was a frightening sight approaching at full speed: a lone rider on a motor-bike. We'd never seen such a powerful machine before. We climbed the stone wall, terrified. The bike-rider was a Rastafarian dressed in black. From afar the machine glinted in the sunlight, dazzling us. 'Black Heart Man, Felix!' I cried. 'Run , run . . .'

We jumped over the wall and hid behind two cotton trees which were whispering in the wind. The bike-rider stopped the engine and hissed air through his teeth loudly. 'Bwoy, de backras dem really brain-wash we peeple; dem frighten of dem own shadow!'

He added: 'Haile Selassie!' Then we heard him revving the engine and he rode off.

'We were hiding from a peaceful Rastaman.' Felix tutted. (The Rastafarian guide at the Green Grotto Lake told us that Rastas were peaceful people.) 'I feel so silly.' The cotton trees were creaking, whispering in the wind. He added: 'Listen, Festus; the trees sound as if they're groaning.'

We were in an abandoned canefield where sugar cane grew wild in the distance. They bent and swayed in the breeze.

'You're right,' I said. 'Let's hurry home.'

We climbed the wall once again and looked up and down the road, choking on the cloud of dust left by the bike-rider.

'I'll race you,' Felix said. 'Then we can go and play. Forget this miserable place.'

When we reached the village square there was a commotion outside Uncle Caesar's shop: the un-employed men gathered round listening to horse racing being broadcast from Caymanas Park in Kingston. My brother Barnaby came out of Uncle Caesar's shop. He sported the latest Tony-C hairstyle: his cropped hair was slicked back at the sides, using hair pomade, and he had a quiff. Father had sent him to buy kerosine oil.

'Did you see the Rastaman on the motor-bike?' we asked.

The men made the motion of jockeys riding runaway horses, whipping. They ignored us. Barnaby said: 'Hush up, boys; can't you see big men listening to horse racing?'

The post mistress closed the post office because it was lunchtime. She smiled at us. 'No Rastaman passed here.'

'He must have!' Felix exclaimed. 'A Rastaman just

69

scared us out at York Castle. Then he shouted "Haile Selassie."'

One of the young men had just returned from Kingston where he'd been working for a 'high-class' family as a yard-boy. He was called Dalbert – Barnaby's best friend. He had told Barnaby that his employers treated him just like a slave. He had made friends with some Rastafarians in Kingston. They had taught him to be proud of his race. He had short dreadlocks. He greeted Barnaby, saying: 'Haile Selassie, King of Kings, Lord of Lords; the Lion of Judah!' (He was acknowledging Haile Selassie as the divine leader of all Rastafarians.)

'Howdy.' Barnaby clapped Dalbert on the back. 'So you've turned a Rasta overnight, eh?'

'Yeah, man.' He ruffled Barnaby's quiff. 'A see yuh sportin' the latest Tony-C hairstyle!'

The village drunk was a small dark-skinned man called Cut-Puss. He wore a pair of flour-bag trousers and old boots without laces. His toes were peeping out of the gaping mouths. He approached Barnaby and Dalbert. 'Oono too fashion-conscious bwoys. Fallah fashion dogs neber drink good soup.'

Barnaby and Dalbert hissed air through their teeth, ignoring Cut-Puss. Meantime there was much excitement going on: the young men crouched and rode the piazza like jockeys whilst listening to the radio. Felix forgot about the bike-rider. He was fascinated by the men's posture. He stood watching them. But I kept wondering what had happened to the stranger. Surely he couldn't have vanished into thin air?

The pastor arrived just as the post mistress was about to go and have lunch at Uncle Caesar's shop. He frowned when she said: 'Festus, forget the bike-rider; he was a duppy-man.'

'Duppy-man?' I narrowed my eyes. 'I saw him from

afar. He was a Rastaman. I glimpsed the hair flying behind him.'

She said, 'Every great house has a ghost. You might have seen the ghost of York Castle: he was a house slave who was in love with the housekeeper. When the backra found out he banished the young man to the field, but field work was too hard for him so he ran away. It is said that he was caught by the overseer, an Englishman, and whipped on that stretch of road where you claimed to have seen the bike-rider. He died of his wounds a few days after the whipping.'

That was news to me. Of course, there were some harsh stories which people chose to forget; this was one such story. I looked at her fair skin and said impatiently, 'I saw a real man on a motor-bike; he wasn't a duppy.'

She said: 'Oh well, if you did see a real man, perhaps he took a different road.'

'There's only one road leading to the village,' I said. 'But if he was a ghost, why would he appear as a Rastaman?'

She said, 'Rastafarianism is a symbol of defiance: in 1935, when I was in my twenties, Mussolini invaded Ethiopia and the great powers ignored Haile Selassie's plea for help. Our people prayed for the deliverance of Ethiopia. They rioted; some rejected Christianity and turned to Ethiopianism, taking Haile Selassie as their God and Marcus Garvey as their prophet. Garvey had prophesied that a king would be crowned in Africa one day: Ras Tafari was crowned Emperor Haile Selassie I.'

The pastor had been listening to the post mistress with one ear, the other listening to the radio. He turned: 'I was a young man in 1930; I was living in Kingston and I remember listening to the BBC World Service broadcasting news of Ras Tafari's coronation:

a black man had been crowned emperor in my lifetime. I felt elated and I was angry when Mussolini invaded Ethiopia. I wanted to take up arms, fight to preserve Ethiopia; the last independent kingdom in Africa.'

Felix had quietly joined us. We stared at the pastor who was speaking with passion: we couldn't imagine him marching off to war; he always preached against violence.

'Are you coming, Barnaby?' I tapped him on the shoulder.

'Can't you see I'm listening to the radio?' he snapped. 'And don't you dare tell Granny Una you've seen me. You know how she feels about gambling, especially on the horses.'

Aunt Esther was standing at the shop door. She frowned at Barnaby. 'Off home with that kerosine oil, young man. Granny Una is waiting on the oil to light the lamps before dusk.'

'See you later, Dalbert.' Barnaby took up the kerosine pan, saying: 'Good day, Aunt Esther, Pastor.' He set off home, not waiting for us.

'I don't know who to pray for first,' the pastor said. 'The young men who condone gambling or the way-ward Rastafarians. Rastafarianism is taking away the young people from the Baptist faith.'

All of a sudden there was a 'vroom, vroom, vroom . . .'

The post mistress looked startled. 'But what is this?'

'Anybody know Dalbert?' A tall thin Rastafarian rode a shiny motor-bike into the village square. All the unemployed men gathered round, admiring the motor-bike. They began to queue up to sit on the machine, revving the engine. The Rastafarian spotted Felix and me. He smiled knowingly. 'A fool yuh bwoys. Wat's all dis nonsense 'bout yuh 'iding under wall from Jah? Me can hide under wall, too, yuh know. Bwoy, country pickneys daft, man.' He greeted Dalbert like an old friend. 'Haile Selassie . . .'

The pastor was annoyed. He went off to Uncle Caesar's shop with the post mistress, grumbling, 'I don't know what this district is coming to! Rastaman trying to convert our well-brought-up children.'

The Rastaman seemed really friendly. Everyone, except Felix and me, touched his dreadlocks and took turns sitting on his bike. Felix and I went home feeling really daft. From that moment we never hid from passing vehicles and, whenever we passed York Castle, we walked with our heads held high.

9

Jack Mandora

Felix and I were so close that whenever he was absent from school I felt like a part of me was missing. Because I was rarely absent Felix never had a chance to miss me. But today he was away because he'd twisted his arm playing cricket. I was wandering in the schoolyard alone, avoiding the cricket pitch, when Mr Lloyd approached me.

'Festus,' he said, 'I gather you don't like cricket?'

I dreaded any conversation with the strict Mr Lloyd. I said, 'I don't hate it, sir. It's just that everyone makes such a fuss when you drop a catch. I get nervous just seeing the ball spinning through the air.'

'Sensitive boy,' he said. 'So you prefer books?'

'Not really, sir,' I said. 'It's just that Mother and Father expect me to do well for Grandfather Cuffee's sake.'

Mr Lloyd smiled. 'I know all about your grandfather: ambitious gentleman; confident public speaker. He would have made a good politician; pity about his lack of education.'

I bore Grandfather Cuffee's shame. He would have me sitting on his knee at six years old reading Bible stories; he knew them all, yet he could just about mark X on the voting list. He died when I was seven years old, making Father promise to educate Barnaby and me.

'Step this way, young man,' Mr Lloyd said. 'I don't usually invite students into my study but you are exceptional. You always conduct yourself in an orderly manner, never rushing headlong into anything. A proper little man, if a child can be classed as such.'

I never really knew why Mr Lloyd singled me out that day. But I was glad because I found myself in a room which smelled of incense. There was a writing desk and a shelf full of books. I developed a liking for the smell of new books from then on. I also liked the large piano and the quill pen on Mr Lloyd's desk. There was a jar of ink and blotting paper there, too. I liked everything about this quiet room.

'This is for you, Festus,' Mr Lloyd said. '*The Oxford Book of Nursery Rhymes*. A friend sent it over from England for me; I'm too old for nursery rhymes. Now, recite that poem you wrote about the bananaman. It is more like a story really.'

'The bananaman is a friend of none,
He has no one at all.
I often wonder what he's done
Or why he seems so small.

Whenever he stops in the village square
Children are instantly afraid
And the adults stand and stare
For the bananaman has been paid.

The bananaman does his shopping
While unemployed men stand looking bored.
One or two youths are bopping
But the bananaman man is ignored.

When finally dusk approaches
The bananaman begins to sing.
He's cheered on by the cockroaches
For, by God, he's their king.'

I finished breathlessly and Mr Lloyd said, 'Poetry

is not just about rhyming. There are other things to take into account. You need to learn the tools of the trade. However, at your age it doesn't matter; imagination is all that counts right now. But some day you're going to make a fine scholar.'

I sniffed the new book passionately, still wondering if I were dreaming. I, Festus, was standing in the dreaded Mr Lloyd's study, and he'd presented me with a book that had come all the way from England. I couldn't believe my luck.

'*Adiós, amigo.*' Mr Lloyd waved a hand. 'Give my regards to your parents. I shall want to speak to them about your future.' He went over to the bookshelf, muttering, 'A few more Grandfather Cuffees in this district and we'd have a school full of promising students.'

But when I arrived home there was bad news. Aunt Hetty had passed away in her sleep in the early hours of the morning and Great-Uncle Lance had died in the afternoon. Mother and Father were busy discussing funeral arrangements for Aunt Hetty. It was Mother's responsibility to see Aunt Hetty to her final resting place properly. Mother was to inherit Aunt Hetty's furniture; the land would go to her brother Ezra who had settled in England. He had written to say England was his home now. He doubted if he would ever return to Jamaica. What had Jamaica done for him? If he'd received a good education he wouldn't be collecting tickets for British Rail.

Father and Uncle Caesar inherited Great-Uncle Lance's property. They would see to the funeral arrangements. Dusk caught my parents deep in discussion: they had to go and lift the mattresses of both old people; their funeral-money would be tucked away there. Mas Rupee and Missis Leena called on us. Missis Leena's first words were: 'Me neber see anythin' like dis before: two old peeple giving up de ghost same day.'

Mas Rupee said, 'De old peeple dem always tek smaddy wid dem fe company. A bet is Aunt Hetty com' li'k dung Mas Lance.'

'They are of the same generation,' Mother said. 'They would have died sooner or later, better they go together.'

'At least they've got company,' Father said.

Felix and I huddled together round the dining-table, watching a peeny-wally buzzing round the kerosine lamp. We fought the tears. We all loved Aunty Hetty and we respected Great-Uncle Lance. He had always been old and ill, and we'd always felt sorry for him: peace, at last.

Granny Una was absent. She and a few of the women of her generation had gone to spend the night at Aunt Hetty's place to keep the lamp burning. Mother handed Father and Mas Rupee a mug of coffee each. The rest of us drank cocoa tea.

'Mek we sen' de old peeple dem off wid a song,' Mas Rupee said. 'No point sittin' 'ere puttin' pressure 'pon we 'ead.'

'Abide with me . . .' Missis Leena led the sing-song.

And so we celebrated the two deaths with songs. Aunt Hetty had left instructions that she wanted to be buried in the churchyard. She didn't want to be alone, on top of the world looking down on the village. Great-Uncle Lance, too, would be buried in the churchyard. Usually people were buried on their properties but, if they had requested it, they could be buried in the churchyard where they'd never be forgotten. And so a joint funeral was arranged.

Felix and I did not attend the funeral because our parents said we would have nightmares. Instead we went up to Aunt Hetty's house and sat under the banyan tree, facing the empty verandah. The rocking-chair had disappeared and there was nothing of Aunt Hetty's presence to cling to. The parakeets that congregated in the banyan tree had taken flight on the day of her death, gone to another village, perhaps.

I handed Felix my penknife. The branches creaked as he carved Great-Uncle Lance and Aunty Hetty's names on the trunk, saying: 'What better place to carve their names. In India the banyan is regarded as a sacred tree. That's what Mama says.'

'I know,' I said. Then I recalled asking Aunt Hetty why the adults danced the quadrille up at her place. She had pointed at the banyan tree, saying: 'If dat banyan tree could talk it would be able to answer yuh question. It's been dere since de days of slavery. It alone knows de trials an' tribulations our peeple suffered at de 'ands of de bakras. Tek a look at de names an' dates carved dere by yuh peeple wheneber suppen important 'appen: Eighteen Thirty-Four . . . Eighteen Sixty-Five, Nineteen-O-Seven, Nineteen Thirty-Eight, Nineteen Forty-Four . . . Nineteen Sixty-Two; Sam Sharpe, Paul Bogle . . .'

I embraced the ancient tree and my heart thumped against the barky trunk. For a second I felt as if the trunk were pulsating. I stroked the bark, saying, 'My navel-string is buried under this tree. Mother said Aunt Hetty had looked after her when she was carrying me. It was a difficult pregnancy and when I was born she insisted on Mother burying my navel-string up here because the banyan is a sacred tree.'

'My navel-string is buried under a fig tree in our yard,' Felix said. 'My very own tree.'

'I can't believe it,' I said. 'Only the other day we were sitting at Aunt Hetty's feet under this tree . . .'

'She was such a wise person,' Felix said. 'Do you remember the time she told us off when we pestered her about the quadrille? She told us off, saying: "Bwoys, time yuh tek frettin' 'bout de quadrille, yuh could be learnin' fe read an' write. We need bright young peeple fe buil' up Jimaica, not loggerheads. Mind yuh noh end up brukin' stones 'cause yuh mek edication pass yuh by de wayside."'

'Yes,' I said. 'Do you remember that terrible quarrel we had about who owned Jamaica: the Arawaks, the English, the Spanish, the Africans or the Asians? Aunt Hetty told us off. She said to me, "Festus, w'en yuh mek up yuh face like dat, yuh resemble yuh gran'puppa, Cuffee." Then she added: "Malice is a bad t'ing, bwoy. Shake 'ands wid Felix an' leave de pas' alone."'

'Mm,' Felix said. 'Let's promise never to quarrel again.'

'Let's shake hands on it,' I said.

The wind howled around us and we sensed the hour had come when Aunt Hetty and Great-Uncle Lance had become branches on the family tree. It was a lonely journey down the hill.

Nine nights after the funerals we attended a wake in honour of Aunt Hetty and Great-Uncle Lance. It was called a set-up. People sat up from dusk until daylight, sending the spirits on their homeward-bound journey in traditional style. After a rousing chorus of 'Guide me, O Thou great Jehovah, pilgrim through this barren land', a traditional nine-night song was sung:

'Coffee ready, carry it come;
Bush tea, put it under table.
If yuh gimme eena condense pan,
Me will set up till part a nite.
But if you gimme eena veedal can,
Me will set up till broad day lite.'

The set-up was held at Aunt Hetty's house where

the adults congregated, talking about how they used to dance the quadrille under Aunt Hetty's guidance. She was a champion quadrille dancer in her day. It was a shame the quadrille would die out with her. Coffee sweetened with condensed milk, and thick slices of bread were passed round. Felix and I were the only children present. We felt proud to have known Aunt Hetty, someone from the old world; a revered old lady. No one was in the mood to dance; they talked about old times. We were all sitting under the banyan tree where a huge bat fluttered overhead, causing one of the villagers to duck: 'A mus' duppy dis; look like Aunt Hetty's spirit com' back a'ready!'

Mr Lloyd attended the wake. He tutted. 'Superstitious mind. Let us hear an Anancy story, lively up this wake. It is what the old lady would have wanted.'

There was a fire near by and the firewood crackled, sending sparks into the air. We sniffed the scent of tobacco.

'A mus' Aunt Hetty a interfere wid de fire, lite 'er pipe.' One of the farmers sniffed. 'Who smoking tobacco?'

No one owned up. The pastor said, 'I suppose it's up to me to uphold tradition: once upon a time, Anancy's wife was working for a rich and wicked old man who wouldn't pay her any money until she could guess his secret name . . .'

'Gwane, pastor!' Mas Rupee said. 'Noh baddah drag yuh wo'ds; yuh know how Aunt Hetty hate peeple draggin' dem wo'ds.'

The pastor continued: 'So one day, Anancy told his wife to dress him up like a baby, sling him on her back and take him to work with her. And she did. When they got to the rich man's house, he was sitting on the verandah rocking and fanning himself. Mrs Anancy asked him if she could leave the baby on the

80

step of the house until she'd finished her work. The rich man agreed and Mrs Anancy set about her work. But the baby kept crying, quietly at first; then louder and louder.

'Anancy's screams attracted the old man's attention. He bent over the baby and Anancy bared his teeth in the old man's face. Well, the old miser was so frightened that he cried out: "Poor me, Seckery. Look wat me live fe see. Young baby wid big mout' full up wid long yellow teeth." He called Mrs Anancy to come and see to her baby. When she came and bent over the baby, Anancy whispered, "'Im name Seckery." So Mrs Anancy was able to guess the miser's name and when he gave her the big bag of money, all the wages owing to her, the baby-Anancy jumped off its back and turned into the man-Anancy. He picked up the bag of money, put it on his back and laughed: "Kya, kya, kya." Jack Mandora me no choose none.'

'What does that mean, Father?' Felix asked.

Everyone burst out laughing: 'Kiff, kiff, kiff . . .'

Mas Rupee was choking himself with laughter. The pastor said, 'It means: "Jack Mandora" – doorman, keeper of heaven's door; "me no choose none" – it is not of my choosing or I take no responsibility for the tales I have told.'

'I see,' Felix said.

The pastor rushed off into another Anancy story and everyone laughed at the tops of their voices. I thought of Aunt Hetty and Great-Uncle Lance, both waiting at heaven's gate to be let in. I prayed that their spirits would find peace. Nonetheless, I was convinced that Aunt Hetty would be restless until Felix and I had gained an education. I had visions of us sucking coarse salt because we'd let education pass us by the wayside. For a moment I was seized with inner panic. I shuddered. I had to succeed, I just had to . . .

81

10

Family Portrait

Felix and I had taken it for granted that the marriage between Matilda and Osman would cement our friendship for ever. How wrong we were. Right now our families weren't speaking, even though Matilda was eight months pregnant. She had quarrelled with Osman, packed her grip and returned home. She had fallen out with Missis Leena, too, which made life difficult for Felix and me. We were expected to take sides. I couldn't go down to Felix's house, and he couldn't come to mine.

The botheration between Matilda and Osman was all to do with Matilda wanting modern things: an oil stove and a kitchen indoors, like the one at the Catholic mission where she used to work. She wanted so many things: a roof of her own, a new bed, the latest candlewick bedspread, even though the climate was so hot, tablecloths... Also, she absolutely refused to labour over a wooden fire with smoke watering her eyes.

Felix liked Matilda a lot. But right now he was annoyed with her. He said she was making Osman's life a misery. Osman couldn't afford a new stove, let alone a house. Where was the money coming from? And then there was the fuss about Matilda turning into a modern woman, copying the style of the women who'd gone abroad, and who now only came home during a crisis: sickness or death. Their hair was straightened. They wore Cutex and lipstick. They wore hobble skirts and slingback, spike-heeled shoes.

Some of the men in the village were worried: their womenfolk were demanding modern things which they couldn't afford; there were lots of squabbles.

Felix's parents had fallen out with my parents over the Osman-Matilda affair. They had expected Mother and Father to march Matilda back home to Osman. But Father said it was up to Matilda and Osman to sort out their problems. Then Granny Una quarrelled with Matilda: she was letting down the family, she should go home to her husband. And when that failed, she threatened to cut Matilda out of her will.

Matilda told Granny Una to go ahead, cut her out of her will: she wasn't exactly looking forward to inheriting threadbare sheets and pillowcases, and she hated chipped china. She wanted new cutlery, crockery, bedlinen. Osman had promised her those things.

Felix and his parents used to call for us on Sunday mornings, on their way to church. But all that stopped; both families were at loggerheads now. It felt really odd to be sitting on opposite sides, different pews, in church. People whispered, nudged each other, shook their heads, but our parents ignored them. Then the pastor reminded Granny Una of her duty as head of the family. Granny Una was vexed because she said no one respected her any more.

The following Sunday, Mas Rupee marched past our gate, Felix walking by his side, head hung low. Missis Leena boldly looked in the direction of our house. She began to sing:

'De shine yeye gal is a trouble to a man,
De shine yeye gal is a trouble to a man . . .
For she want an' she want an' she want
eberything . . .'

Granny Una was putting on her shoes. She looked up.

'Missis Leena, tedday is Sunday. Yuh cahn sing jamma on de Sabbath day, yuh 'ear me!'

Missis Leena said, 'It seems yuh cahn control yuh fambily, Mama. So no baddah try fe control me, mam!'

'Matilda, yuh see wat yuh done now?' Granny Una said. 'Not a soul 'ave any respec' fe me . . .'

Matilda was cutexing her fingernails. She waved at Missis Leena. 'Morning, Mother.'

Missis Leena flounced off. My parents came out on to the verandah. Mother sighed and said, 'Festus, fetch my Bible and hymn book, son. No need to hurry. We don't want to catch up with Rupee and Lois, not in their mood.'

Granny Una pursed her lips. Father said, 'Not another word, Mama.'

Felix and I always walked home from school together. But that Monday evening our friendship ended temporarily when Felix announced, 'Mama says Matilda is spoilt and selfish.'

I was annoyed. I said, 'Matilda has a right to expect nice things. Osman promised . . .'

We were walking along the dusty main road where reeds grew thick on the stone walls. A lone vulture swooped and landed on a sickly-looking cow-calf in the pasture. Felix turned to me and said, 'Your parents have spoilt Matilda, Festus. She expects everything to be in tip-top condition.'

It seems we're taking sides now, Felix,' I said.

'I'm not,' he replied. 'You are. I just don't like to see Mama and Papa so upset, not to mention Osman.'

I said, 'And I don't like to see Granny Una so upset, let alone Mother and Father.'

Felix had had enough. He looked really upset. He kicked a pebble and said, 'I'm fed up of you, Festus.

I'm going to tell Mama that you've been cussing me.'
He ran off.

When I reached Felix's gate Missis Leena was waiting for me. (Felix was nowhere to be seen.) She said: 'Festus, a dohn want yuh upsettin' Felix, yuh 'ear me?'

'Yes, Missis Leena.' I went home, sulking.

At suppertime we sat on the verandah drinking cocoa tea and eating crackers as usual. I told the family about the fuss with Felix. Buster growled, peeny-wallies lit up the verandah and an owl hooted in the trees. Mother and Father drank their cocoa tea, pondering.

Granny Una slurped her tea and said, 'Matilda, pack up yuh troubles an' go for a dohn like yuh style.'

Matilda sat with her legs stretched out on a chair. She said, 'Grandpa Cuffee made this house for me, too. I don't have to go if I don't want to.'

Father lost his temper. He brushed a peeny-wally off his arm roughly. 'Matilda, you gave up your right to this house when you chose a husband. I am no longer responsible for you.'

Matilda cried, 'Everybody is against me, even you, Father.' She rose and went into the sitting room, puffing.

Mother rose and said, 'Matilda is nearing her time. We mustn't upset her too much.' She went to comfort her.

'Salvan,' Granny Una said, 'dis nonsense 'as to stop.' She looked into the house, adding: 'Where is Barnaby? A cahn see dat young man nowadays; a wahn me smellin' salt.'

Barnaby was in the bedroom we shared, getting dressed to go up to the village square to play draughts with Dalbert.

Matilda came out on to the verandah with Mother.

She said: 'I'm sorry, Father, Granny, but I'm not going back until Osman finds somewhere for us to live.'

Granny Una said, 'Ah, Matty. Patience is a virtue.'

'Salvan,' Mother said, 'we must give them a quarter-acre of land; we must.'

'Not ober me dead body,' Granny Una said. 'Me dear Cuffee inherited dat land, to be passed on to 'im male 'eirs.'

Father snapped: 'I can't stand botheration! Matilda, I'm taking you home now!'

There was a scatter rug on the floor. Granny Una had made it from two hessian sacks sewn together, feeding bits of coloured material through the back, then pulling them through the front. Matilda was wearing flip-flops. She had one foot tucked under the edge of the rug. She rose and said, 'You'll have to carry me home, Father.' She stormed off, catching one of her flip-flops in the rug. She tripped and fell.

'Lawd a macy,' Granny Una wailed. 'Matty tumble dung. Jesus wept.' She sprang to her feet, dropping the enamel mug.

For a moment my parents looked as if they had been caught in slow motion. They just stood there gaping.

'Dohn jus' stan' dere, Salvan an' Lois,' Granny Una said.

'The baby is coming,' Matilda groaned.

My parents snapped out of their trance. Father almost tripped over the rug. He bent and rolled it up. Mother took it indoors. Granny Una sat on the floor, comforting Matilda.

'Barnaby,' Father shouted, 'go and fetch Nurse.'

Granny Una said, 'Salvan, de nurse lives ober t'ree miles away. No. We haffe deliver de baby ourself.'

Mother came out on to the verandah, saying:

'Festus, go and tell Missis Leena and Mas Rupee the news, hurry.'

Father helped Matilda indoors and Granny Una went off to boil hot water, saying: 'Festus, tell Missis Leena to let yuh sleep over; dis is no place fe a man-child.'

Barnaby came out on to the verandah wearing a calypso shirt and there was a striped handkerchief sticking out of his trouser pocket. He said, 'Trust Matilda to spoil my evening.'

Father said, 'Barnaby, go and tell Osman that Matilda is in labour. Then you can go and stay overnight with Mas Ivan and Dalbert. This is going to be a long night.'

It was dusk and the peeny-wallies lighted the way as I rushed down to Felix's house, no longer afraid of duppies, wondering whether Missis Leena would turn me away. When she heard the news she said, 'Poor Matty, de chile gwine need me support.' She rushed off into the night, telling Felix to make room in his bed for me.

Felix and I sat on the verandah with Mas Rupee, dispute forgotten. We sat wondering where babies came from. Mas Rupee sat smoking a pipe. Father and Osman arrived, saying Granny Una had banished them. It was going to be a dark night. There was no light on the verandah. The men reminisced about when we boys were born, a few days apart: how they'd congregated first on Mas Rupee's verandah, followed by Father's verandah.

'Fancy Matilda tumbling down like that,' Father said.

Osman shot up. 'Wat, yuh mean fe seh Matty tumble dung? Poor love, a should go to 'er.' He sounded distraught.

'Tan tuddy, son.' Mas Rupee poured Osman a glass

87

of rum, adding: 'Felix, yuh an' Festus should be drawin' snore now. Off to bed, bwoys. Day soon lite.'

Next morning we woke with the news that Matilda had had a baby girl, whom she and Osman named Joy. Granny Una insisted that Matilda stayed in bed for seven days. On the eighth day both families crowded on to the verandah admiring the new baby. Felix and I liked the name Joy because the baby reunited both families, a joyous occasion. Granny Una insisted on wetting the baby's head, the mole, with rum. But there was still the little problem of Matilda not wanting to live with her in-laws.

Father said, 'Matilda, Rupee and I have the perfect solution to your problem: we are going to buy you and Osman Aunt Hetty's cottage. Both of you can leave us in peace then.'

'But it belongs to Uncle Ezra,' Matilda said. 'What if he doesn't want to sell it?'

'Aha.' Mother waved an airmail letter. 'Ezra wrote some time ago and asked me to sell the land. I just didn't mention it to you children. He says England is his home now. He has no intention of coming back to Jamaica.'

'De man forget where 'im navel-string bury,' Granny Una said. 'Fancy telling yuh to sell fambily lan', Lois.' She turned to Father and Mas Rupee: 'Bwoys, keep yuh money. A have a likkle money save up. Since Cuffee never believe in girl pickneys inheriting lan', only bwoy pickneys, a vow to give Matilda something myself.'

Matilda said: 'Thank you, Granny. I'm sorry for what I said about your sheets and pillowcases; I do want them really.'

'Eberybaddy throw a likkle temper tantrum now an' den, chile,' Granny Una said. 'But from tedday a wahn yuh fe put yours aside. No more coming back 'ome, yuh 'ear me?'

'Yes, Granny.' Matilda turned to Osman. 'Forgive?'

'Nothing to forgive,' Osman said. 'I love you.'

'I love you, too.' Matilda and Osman kissed each other.

Felix and I didn't know where to look. Mother, Father and Mas Salvan smiled. Missis Leena clapped. 'Praise de Lawd.'

Granny Una said, 'Amen.'

The tiny baby with the shock of black hair went from hand to hand, meeting her new family. Osman took her eagerly, saying, 'Little one, what can I give you? I promise . . .'

'Osman,' Mas Rupee interrupted. 'Not another promise.'

Everyone laughed. Then Mother began to comb Matilda's hair. Granny Una's ears perked up. She looked towards the gate when Buster began to bark. She said, 'But see yah!'

There was Barnaby coming up the path with a young lady. Father cleared his throat. Mas Rupee blinked. Missis Leena said, 'Dis is wat yuh call a modern gal, Matty. Yes, mam.'

Barnaby sought Granny Una's approval. First thing he said was: 'Good day, Granny. This is my girlfriend, Janey Morris.'

'Eh-eh.' Granny Una buttoned her cardigan. 'Barnaby, tan tuddy, boasty-bwoy. Yuh mean fe seh yuh forsake yuh granny fe smaddy else?' she joked, calming Barnaby's nerves.

'No, Granny,' he said. 'I still love you, but . . .'

Janey was a pretty girl in a sleeveless, floral shift and slingback shoes. Her hair was straightened and styled in what she later called 'a French pleat'. She wore lipstick and Cutex on her fingernails. She had come to the village to teach at our school, she was boarding with Mr Lloyd and his wife, the deputy headmistress whom we called Aunt Isabelle.

'Good afternoon, everyone,' Janey said. 'Mr and Mrs Lloyd send congratulations to the new parents and grandparents.'

Granny Una said: 'An' wat about de great-gran'maddah?'

'You, too,' Janey said hastily.

'Come on up on to the verandah, my dear.' Mother liked the newcomer straight away. 'A teacher, eh?'

Missis Leena said: 'Matty, fancy me did a mek-mek seh yuh too modern. A 'ope yuh not bearin' me a grudge, daughter?'

'No, Mother.' Matilda smiled at Missis Leena.

Two new members joined the family: Joy and Janey. It was a tight squeeze to fit everyone on to the verandah, not forgetting Buster. The dog sat at Janey's feet, wagging its tail while Barnaby stood proudly at her side. Osman handed baby Joy to Granny Una who promptly sat in Aunt Hetty's rocking-chair which she'd inherited. Father and Matilda stood on either side of Granny Una, four generations of the same family. Granny Una cooed: 'Joy-Joy, yuh need a brother now.'

Mother said, 'Perfect picture. Don't move. I'm going to get my charcoal and that large sheet of drawing paper I've been saving for that special occasion.'

Mother went indoors. Felix and I stared from Joy to Matilda. We said in unison: 'Where do babies come from?'

There was a kind of hush.

'Festus, Felix,' Granny Una said, 'dere's a time an' place fe eberything, bwoys; yuh 'ear me?'

'Yes, Granny,' we muttered. 'Big people never give a straight answer.'

All was forgotten when Mother returned. She wanted to sketch the whole family, just the outline for now. Somehow she was going to include herself later. The good thing was that several sittings were required. The family would be together often in the days ahead. Felix and I sat at Granny's feet. Everyone crowded into the picture, even Janey. And as Mother stood back sketching, I realised it was the first time she had ever drawn real people. I was so proud of her, I had to force my face not to break into a smile. I wondered what the picture would look like in colour. I made a vow that one day I would buy Mother a set of paint brushes, sketchpads, an easel and different-coloured paints.

11

The Bananaman

Felix had once said nature was very cruel, and I had to agree with him. As if the passing of Aunt Hetty and Great-Uncle Lance wasn't enough, we were now mourning the loss of Mr Lloyd. He died of a heart attack before you could say 'Jack Mandora'. But not before he'd spoken to my parents at Joy's christening (a quiet affair because Osman insisted on footing the bill himself). He told them that I 'showed promise' and should be tutored for the Common Entrance Examination.

The new headmistress was Mr Lloyd's widow, Aunt Isabelle. My parents were paying for me to have extra lessons after school with Aunt Isabelle. She was a plump woman whose fingers were always stained with ink. She lived in a blue and white cottage, adjoining the school. I often sat in the cool lounge-diner, where a Welsh dresser displayed plain china, revising for the Common Entrance Exam which was equivalent to the eleven-plus. People said it was harder than the eleven-plus, in order to prevent children of working-class background from gaining access to secondary education.

I felt really guilty because Felix was not with me. Children had to be rigorously tutored for the CEE, and that cost money. Mas Rupee had said he couldn't afford to pay for extra lessons because he didn't have 'a red cent in the bank'.

'Put your books away, Festus,' Aunt Isabelle said one evening. We were sitting in the study. She lifted the lid of the piano. 'All work and no play makes Jack a dull boy.' She missed Mr Lloyd dreadfully. I, too, missed Mr Lloyd in his squeaky-brown shoes. Aunt Isabelle played the piano and sang: 'Every time I remember Liza, water come a me eye . . .' She stopped playing the piano, took a deep breath. 'I can't get over Lloydie's death, Festus; it was so sudden. I know he was strict on the children, but that was his style: he wanted the children to fear him, if it meant they would study harder, do well in school.'

It was the first time I'd heard Mr Lloyd being addressed in such loving terms. I said, 'I understand, Aunt Isabelle.'

She lowered the lid of the piano. 'Festus, from the first day you started school, Lloydie said you showed promise; "a talented boy". He never singled you out in the classroom because he knew you were sensitive.'

'But why did he have to single out Felix? I asked. 'He always made Felix forget what he'd learnt.'

'Lloydie singled out many children, Festus,' she said. 'Felix excelled himself on the cricket pitch; Lloydie wanted to see if he could excel himself in the classroom, too.'

'I used to be frightened of him.' I looked around the study, taking in the writing desk. Everything had remained the same. 'I just wished he hadn't singled out Felix so often.'

She rubbed her swollen eyelids. 'From what Lloydie told me, Felix is a talented boy. But he places too much emphasis on sport, less on his books. Hopefully, one day he will excel himself in the classroom, too.'

When she put it like that, I stopped fretting about how unfair Mr Lloyd had been to Felix. Perhaps he was trying to help him, though he certainly went about it the wrong way.

'Think what it would mean to your parents and Lloydie if you won a scholarship, Festus,' Aunt Isabelle said. 'If it's the last thing I do, I'm going to develop your talent.'

'What is my talent, Aunt Isabelle?' I asked.

It seemed Aunt Isabelle didn't want me to become too sure of myself. She smiled radiantly. 'Well, Festus, I know you have a talent, but it is hidden at the moment.'

'Felix is very talented,' I said. 'He's a good cricketer and he can draw. I hope he gets to go to art school one day.'

Aunt Isabelle said: 'I hope so, too. But right now opportunity is knocking for you, Festus. Grasp it while you can; concentrate on your studies and stop worrying about Felix. You'll make new friends when you go to high school.'

I knew that was the end of the conversation where Felix was concerned. Then I began to worry about the competition between the two schools which was not only in the field of sport. Both schools wanted to produce a crop of children who'd go to high schools in Kingston, taking the school's reputation with them. I just didn't want to be in competition with anyone. What if I failed? No! I had to succeed for the sake of my family. I gathered up my books. 'Good evening, Aunt Isabelle.'

The following day was Saturday. It was the only time Felix and I spent together now. We went down to the banana-walk, a damp, dark place where Mas Rupee cultivated bananas. He had hired extra hands to help him gather the bananas, even though he'd said he couldn't really afford to pay them.

The men were taking a break, and when I saw Felix laughing gaily with them, I felt so jealous. He was enjoying himself without me, he hadn't missed me. I felt sad at the thought of Felix making friends with anyone but me.

> 'Jackass wid him long tail,
> Bag a coco comin' down.
> Jackass wid him long tail,
> Bag a coco comin' down . . .'

The men had been sitting on the ground singing. They stopped, rose and dusted off their clothes. Then they resumed cutting down bunches of bananas. There was a mouldy scent in the air. The banana leaves hung limply as if their wings had been broken.

Felix rose and caught a caterpillar crawling on a banana leaf. He said, 'Soon you'll be a beautiful butterfly.'

'How can you bear to touch it, Felix?' I watched a green lizard crawling up the trunk of a banana tree.

He put it down and caught a butterfly. 'The caterpillar turns into this beautiful creature, Festus. One day I'm going to draw them all.' He let the butterfly flutter away.

We were lost in a maze of banana trees which towered above us. The red earth was damp under our feet, birds sang gaily, beetles searched for food and the scent of gum invaded our nostrils; a gooey substance oozed from the banana trees, weeping for the hands of bananas which had been cut down.

'Felix,' I said, 'how would you feel if I had to go away? Mother and Father want me to go to secondary school in Town.'

He looked at me and said, 'Do you remember the time when we went to Green Grotto Lake? The pastor hinted then that we'd have to part one day. It's happening now, Festus.'

'I never want to be separated from you, not ever,' I said.

'Me neither,' Felix said.

'Then why don't you plead with your parents to let you study with me, Felix?'

He watched a snail crawling on the damp earth. 'It's no use, Festus. Papa wants me to help him on the banana plantation because he can't really afford hired hands and he hasn't got the money to pay for private lessons for me.'

'It's all so unfair,' I said. 'Why is Mas Rupee so mean? Why can't he be like Father?'

'Your parents are lucky, Festus,' he said. 'They've both inherited debt-free legacies, unlike us. Father has only just managed to pay off the land we've lived on all these years. He says Grandfather Chen was always in court, suing people for this and that. The land was heavily mortgaged, and with all those lawsuits which Grandfather lost, Father inherited a lot of debts. He can't afford hired hands because all the profit goes on paying wages instead of debts.'

I had always taken it for granted that everyone owned debt-free land. 'I'm going to deliberately fail the exam, Felix. That way we can both work with your father on the banana plantation.'

'That's a wicked thing to say,' Felix said. 'What about your parents, all that money? How could you say such a thing?'

Felix seemed so wise then. He made me feel foolish. He thought of things which never crossed my mind and he was beginning to act like a big man.

'I thought we were best friends, Felix?' I rose. 'But you're acting as if our friendship means nothing to you.'

'Of course it does,' he said. 'It's just that I don't want to take the CEE. I don't want to put my parents into debt on my account. They have enough of that already. Besides, it isn't as if I'm leaving school. I'm going to take the JSC when I'm fourteen. Aunt Isabelle spoke to Father the other day. She said I could study in the evenings with her – once the CEE is over – in return for a hand of bananas or a hand of yam as payment. Father agreed, Festus.'

'But you can't take the Jamaica School Certificate until you are sixteen,' I said.

'Aunt Isabelle says I'm bright enough to take it at fourteen,' Felix said. 'She's going to enter me.'

'But you're only eleven now,' I cried. 'Fourteen is a long way off. You won't be able to go to high school in Kingston with me. We're going to be separated.'

'What must be, must be.' Felix watched an army of cockroaches circling a discarded, decaying ripe banana.

'Don't give up so easily, Felix,' I said. 'Where there's a will, there's a way; you know that.'

'There's no other way, Festus,' Felix said. 'But don't worry. When Father pays off his debts everything will be OK.'

Mas Rupee arrived. He inspected the green bananas which were to be shipped abroad. 'Felix, gimme a 'and, bwoy. Dere's a lot of roaches crawlin' roun' an' me noh want dem crawlin' over me bananas.'

'So that's where you got the idea for your poem, "The Bananaman", from, Festus?' Felix said.

Mas Rupee turned to me. 'Festus, me not no king o'de cockroaches. Me is king o' de castle. Dohn stan' up dere like no big shot, bwoy. Come an' soil yuh 'ands eena de red dirt.'

'Papa,' Felix said. 'You know Missis Lois doesn't like Festus working on the land.'

'Wat de eyes dohn see, de 'eart cahn feel.' Mas Rupee bent over a bunch of bananas. 'Festus, if yuh gwine write 'bout yuh peeple, yuh haffe capture dem voice. Dat poem too Englishy fe me; yuh haffe recite it eena patwa.'

The workmen had overheard the conversation. They joined us, laughing. Next thing I found myself working side by side with Felix and Mas Rupee, reciting my poem in patois. The workmen soon learned the lines. While they cut down bunches of bananas, they recited my poem. One of them shouted: 'Suppose we buck up duppies eena de banana-walk? Dem mus' frighten fe 'ear poetry instead of jamma.'

12

The Lucky Ones

The morning of the school examination saw me on bended knees. Granny Una woke before the cock began to crow. She insisted on us all kneeling down at my bedside, praying. Her voice filled the semi-darkness where the kerosine lamp burned low.

'Papa God, I beseech yuh: let yuh lite shine on yuh chosen one's forehead today. Give Festus courage dat he may face de first 'urdle in 'im young life . . .'

'Amen,' Father said. 'Dear Lord, go with Festus this morning. Send your angels to guide him throughout the day . . .'

'Amen.' Mother took up the prayer. 'Father, give Festus wisdom, knowledge and understanding; guide his hands . . .'

The morning breeze broke the dawn, causing the lamp to flicker. Granny Una said, 'T'ank yuh, Papa God. Yuh give us a sign. A gwine keep dis lamp burnin' all day fe Festus!'

After a breakfast of afu yams, boiled green bananas and calloo, to keep my strength up during the examination, Granny Una hung a crucifix round my neck for God's protection. Father put an old horseshoe in my satchel. Mother made the sign of the cross on my forehead; everyone wished me luck.

Mas Rupee, Missis Leena, Felix, Matilda, Osman and Joy came to wish me luck, too. Then Mas Rupee said: 'Do, Festus; no baddah go eena exam go splash ink 'pon de paper or siddung deh mek up yuh face like yuh fo-fool. Try fe wo'k out de answers 'pon scrap paper.'

Missis Leena said: "'Ere Festus, me lucky rabbit foot. It will bring yuh luck; it neber fail.'

Felix gave me a wishbone. 'Break it with me, Festus, and make a wish.' We did.

Matilda and Osman said, 'We have nothing to give you, Festus. Just keep a steady head.'

Barnaby stood at Granny Una's side smiling. He said: 'Festus, say howdy-do to Janey for me, and good luck.'

I thanked everyone. Then I was overcome with a terrible weight. I felt weighed down with the good-luck charms as I stuffed them into my brown satchel. I just couldn't fail. I had always lived in dread of failure, especially since that cricket match when I was ten years old.

Father brought his dapple-grey mare, Jessie, round to the verandah and set me upon the horse. 'Son, ride like a man today.' He stood alongside and we set off, looking ahead.

We travelled along the dusty road where reeds grew on bankings. The horse's hoofs made such a racket that I could hear the echo from afar. I looked down and said, 'Oh, Father, what if I fail? I couldn't bear to let you all down. What would become of me then?'

'Life's journey is just beginning for you, son,' Father said. 'Don't falter along the way. Faith is the key to every door. Come, come. Don't use that word "failure" again!'

We met other parents taking their children to school to sit the dreaded CEE. What surprised me was the amount of fathers who'd turned out; many dreaded the thought of their sons working alongside them in the fields. My heart missed a beat when I thought of Felix. Then I thought of Aunt Hetty, how she'd warned us about not letting education pass us by the wayside. I prayed silently that it wouldn't pass Felix by.

Father set me down at the school gate and I said, 'My legs are trembling, Father. I can't walk.'

The mare's rump trembled and she swished her tail, almost knocking me down. Father laughed. 'See, Festus. Even Jessie is chastising you. Now: shoulders back, head high and whistle a happy tune.' He made to leave without wishing me luck. He had to get back to look after the animals.

'Don't go, Father,' I said. 'Please stay a while.'

'I'll come and collect you later, son.' Father greeted the other farmers, then mounted Jessie. He clip-clopped off home on the mare. I thought of Felix then. We should have been taking the exam together. I couldn't bear the thought of him not being by my side and I blinked several times. I felt so alone! But when I looked around the schoolyard, the other parents were leaving and the children all looked equally afraid: we had to succeed because education was our only way out of rural Jamaica.

'You afraid?' The question was addressed to no one in particular. Children began to group together, sharing their sense of fear. 'Nope,' came a few quaking voices; I was shocked to hear my own voice. No one wanted to admit that they were suffering from nerves.

The bell rang and everyone jumped to attention. The few remaining parents stood, mumbling last-minute prayers.

The school seemed so bare: the blackboards had been removed and the desks and chairs stood in single rows. Meantime the teachers, including Miss Janey Morris (I forgot Barnaby's message), stood up front, at the head of each row, looking really serious. The papers were handed out and we were told to settle ourselves and check our pens and pencils.

'Good morning, children.' Aunt Isabelle read the rules: 'Don't speak to your neighbours, don't display any bad habits, like sniffing or humming, and good luck!'

All of a sudden I was overcome with nerves and, when we were told to turn over our papers, my hands shook like Great-Uncle Lance's used to. I thought of him then. How he used to say, 'Bwoys, is weh dem teaching oono a school . . .' And then I turned over my paper: how I hated arithmetic. I turned down the paper and looked to Aunt Isabelle for guidance: a smile, a nod. She never looked in my direction once. I thought of Felix; if only he were here now. I began to write furiously, calculating fractions and algebra with anger boiling up.

'Stop!' Aunt Isabelle's voice rang out. 'Time for the next paper, history, followed by English . . .'

Throughout the ordeal, Aunt Isabelle stood on the platform, hands behind her back, staring ahead. Despite Aunt Isabelle laying down the rules, children fidgeted and sniffed, though no one hummed, and the time flew away from us.

'Stop writing and put your pens down!' Aunt Isabelle ordered. 'Time up.'

The papers were gathered up in silence. Then each teacher walked alongside a row, handing out a paradise-plum sweet.

'What's this in aid of?' the children asked.

Aunt Isabelle looked down from the platform. 'Sweeties from Mr Lloyd. He had been planning to give all of you a paradise-plum sweet upon completion of the examination. He had a little speech ready, too. "Savour this moment because it will determine your future."' And with that she hastily left the hall without saying another word.

We sniffed, almost choking on the sweets. Mr Lloyd had left us all a little something. He was indeed a special teacher. He cared about us to his dying day. Some children rushed out of the school, eager to tell parents and friends how they'd done. Others strolled out in silence, fretting as if the examination was about to begin all over again. I strolled out in a sombre mood, for I was recalling Mr Lloyd's office: his desk, his books. He had gone, but we hadn't forgotten him on this crucial day; he made sure of it. I savoured the last of my paradise-plum sweet and joined Father.

'Not a word, Festus,' he said. 'It is bad luck to discuss the examination. Cheer up. We're going up to Aunt Hetty's cottage to have a picnic with Osman and Matilda.'

'Will Felix be there?' I asked.

'Of course,' Father said. 'Missis Leena and your mother have been planning this surprise for days.'

'What if I don't pass, Father?' I said.

'Faith, Festus, faith!' He helped me to mount Jessie.

Many parents and children were to wish that afternoon had lasted for ever. A few weeks later we gathered in the school on a Thursday evening to hear Aunt Isabelle and Mr Llewelyn jointly read out the names of the successful candidates from both schools. We waited in anticipation to hear the names of the lucky ones. 'Bustamante House: Brian James, Ephraim Tucker, Dora Johnston. Norman Manley House: Festus . . .'

'Yes, sir!' Father clapped me on the back. 'Well done.'

'T'ank you, Papa God!' Granny Una cried. 'Me did t'ink seh Festus let we dung – de only one from Norman Manley House.'

'Aunt Hetty can rest in peace now, Festus,' Mother

said seriously. 'Well done, son.'

'Me did know seh de bwoy wouldn't let we dung,' Missis Leena said. 'Not wid me lucky rabbit foot an' all.'

Mas Rupee said, 'Congratulations, bwoy! Ah cahn wait fe 'ear Felix name call out w'en 'im pass de JSC.'

Felix and I sat there, quietly observing weeping parents and children, the losers. I sensed that Felix would have given anything to share the stage with me. I was one of the lucky ones, but I just couldn't savour the moment; I would have given anything to have heard Felix's name called that day.

13

Partners

This was to be the last term Felix and I would ever sit side by side in a classroom. We wanted so much to make the most of our time together, help each other to overcome obstacles. Felix hated mathematics; I made it my job to help him with algebra, LCMs, long division. Felix insisted I mastered the game of cricket, much as I hated it. Mr Lloyd had once said that if you wanted to elevate yourself you had to master the sport of the élite: cricket. So Felix and I spent our last term complementing each other like never before.

Despite the emphasis placed on education, the will to succeed, what Felix and I liked most about school was the annual concert which marked the end of the school term. This year it was to be held at Bustamante House. The schoolyard was littered with plum trees. Behind the school you looked down on a gully, full of cedar trees, where a cricket pitch was marked out in the red soil. The smell of cedar mingled with that of freshly cut grass and the scent of decaying windfall plums as you entered the schoolyard.

This year the concert was extra special because Felix and I were to recite the story of Joseph. We had been practising our lines with Aunt Isabelle who had warned us not to let her down. It was bad enough, so many children failing the CEE, she couldn't stand a lapse of memory from us right now.

Mr Llewelyn had insisted there should be a joint concert, taking the strain off Aunt Isabelle who was still mourning the loss of Mr Lloyd. She really needed cheering up. Everyone missed Mr Lloyd, even the children from Bustamante House who all knew him. He used to stop any child he met out of school hours, along the road. 'You, there, halt: what do the initials AD, BC and QC stand for?'

The girls from Bustamante House wore navy pleated uniforms and white blouses while the girls from our school wore green pleated uniforms; all boys wore khaki uniforms. But the girls who were taking part in the concert came in national costume: plaid skirts, red puffed-sleeved blouses and plaid headscarves.

Because the concert was so well attended, it was held in the schoolyard. The school served as an Adventist church on Saturdays so there was a baptismal pool in one corner of the yard. The sickly sweet smell of fermenting plums invaded our nostrils as Aunt Isabelle and Mr Llewelyn herded the younger children round a concrete area near the pool, a kind of patio which served as the stage. The piano was brought out and Aunt Isabelle and Mr Llewelyn took turns playing it. The sun shone down on us and the adults perspired, fanned themselves, chased flies and slapped mosquitoes which sung round their ears or bit their arms and legs.

The concert began with the national pledge: 'Before God and all mankind, I pledge my love and loyalty in the service of Jamaica'; the singing of the national song: 'Jamaica, Jamaica, Land We Love . . .', followed by a recitation, honouring our national flower. We all recited 'Now the Lignum Vitae Blows' by Tom Redcam. Felix and I sat up front, reciting along with the younger children, who stood by the piano fidgeting as they recited.

The recitation ended. Then a group of boys and

girls stepped forward. One of the boys began to sing and a chorus of voices responded in harmony: 'A chi-chi bud oh . . .'

'Encore, encore!' The applause was deafening at the end of the performance. Everyone repeated: 'A chi-chi bud oh!'

Now it was time for Felix and me to read the story of Joseph. We stood by the piano coyly, and Mas Rupee and Missis Leena, shouted, 'Gwane, bwoys. 'Old oono heads up.'

Felix recited: 'Jacob was a rich man who had twelve sons. He owned many sheep and cows. But Joseph was his favourite son and Jacob didn't mind the others knowing this . . .'

I took over saying, 'But the others were jealous of Joseph, who had strange dreams which he couldn't understand; he told his brothers, saying how in one dream they were all binding sheaves of corn at harvest-time and their sheaves bowed down to his sheaves.'

Felix cleared his throat. 'The brothers were really angry. They snapped, "Are you trying to tell us that one day we shall all bow down and worship you?"'

I was no longer feeling bashful. I said confidently, 'Well, in another dream Joseph dreamt that the sun, the moon and the stars all bowed down and worshipped him.'

Felix was beginning to enjoy the story, too. He told how the brothers were sent to a far-off place, Shechem, to mind the sheep and Jacob was anxious when they did not return home. He sent Joseph to find them. But they were nowhere to be found. A stranger said they had gone to another place to find fresh grass. Joseph went looking for them. When the brothers saw him coming they said, 'Here comes the dreamer!' They hated Joseph and plotted to murder him.

'Reuben was one of the brothers,' I said. 'He begged mercy for Joseph. He told his brothers not to soil their hands with his blood. So they sold him to some passing Ishmaelites for twenty pieces of silver. They took his multi-coloured coat and stained it with blood. Then they took it home to Jacob.'

By then everyone was emotional, shaking their heads, sighing and encouraging Felix to speak up. He said, 'Jacob looked at the blood-drenched coat and wept, saying a wild beast had killed Joseph. He cried "Oh, my son, my son!"'

Aunt Isabelle was still sitting at the piano. She took over. 'Many years later there was famine in the land and the brothers went to Egypt looking for food. Joseph was a great man by then. It was his job to make sure that everyone got their fair share of food. His brothers came and bowed down before him, begging for food. The dream had been fulfilled.'

'Joseph forgave his brothers and sent for his parents to come and live in Egypt,' Mr Llewelyn said. 'The children of Israel had found a new land.'

There was no applause. The adults shook their heads. 'Ah, sah: broddas sell dem own brodda eena slavery, imagine!'

A cloud of sadness descended. Mr Llewelyn clapped. 'Time for some real entertainment. A concert just wouldn't be the same without a little something from our very own Miss Lou.'

Louise Bennett was a famous Jamaican comedian whom we called 'Miss Lou'. She lived in Kingston and we'd never seen her, but everyone said she was plump and wore national costume. We thought of her always in a plaid skirt, red puffed-sleeved blouse and plaid headdress, and lots of bangles on her wrists. We'd heard her reciting her poems in patois over the radio. We had no trouble memorising these poems which were about the daily life of Jamaicans. Since politics was a serious issue in Jamaica, everyone loved Miss Lou's poem 'Rightful Way' which seemed to be making fun of voters and politicians alike.

The educated members of our village spoke what they called 'proper English' while most of the villagers spoke patois. Granny Una and Felix's parents refused to speak anything but patois; they were really proud of the mother tongue. Mas Rupee had once rebuked one of the villagers who'd just returned from England: 'Do massa, mind yuh noh bite yuh tongue, 'bout yuh a put it between yuh teet'. Me noh care 'bout noh foreign twang. Me satisfy wid me patwa, bredda.'

We had never heard Aunt Isabelle speak in patois. She said: 'We got the vote in 1944, Miss Lou wrote several poems about the dilemma of voting day – who to vote for?' She recited 'Rightful Way':

'Cous weh fe do me shame o' yuh!
Yuh mean yuh such a goat!
Yuh mean yuh got so much big chat
An doan know how fe vote . . .

Yuh doan haffe cross out nutten
Nor haffe draw no line,
Jus mark a X side o' de name
A who deh pon yuh mine . . .'

'Gwane, gal!' The villagers applauded and laughed uncontrollably. 'Patwa is a part of we 'eritage! God bless Miss Lou. She mek edicated negya proud of dem maddah tongue.'

Mr Llewelyn applauded. 'For she's a jolly good fellow, for she's a jolly good fellow . . . and so say all of us.'

'Three cheers for Miss Lou!' The adults applauded. 'Hip, hip, hooray . . . She carry de maddah tongue

109

abroad, unlike many edicated Jamaicans who 'fraid fe speak patwa at 'ome.'

Everyone laughed, even Mr Llewelyn who never spoke in patois. But he was not alone. My parents had received very little education but they forsook patois, saying: 'Festus, you must learn to dance at home before you can dance abroad.'

Finally the concert drew to a close and we sang a song which told the story of a self-proclaimed prophet called Bedward who lived in Kingston. He believed that he could cure illness by baptising the sufferer in the Hope River. We never knew whether he cured anyone but we could imagine his followers, all dressed in white, being dunked in the river fully clothed. We were standing by the pool in which sinners were baptised; we sang eagerly:

'Dip dem, Bedward, dip dem,
Dip dem in de healing stream . . .'

'Come, Isabelle,' Mr Llewelyn said. 'Mek we dip an' fall, missis; show dese peeple seh we noh forget weh we comin' fram.'

This was the best concert Felix and I had ever attended. The cricket match had been cancelled because of Mr Lloyd's untimely death.

Mr Llewelyn dipped Aunt Isabelle, who fell back in a kind of mock baptism, while everyone sang: 'Dip dem, Bedward, dip dem, dip dem in de healing stream . . .'

Aunt Isabelle cheered up, forgetting her troubles, and I sensed that the days of rivalry were over; a new partnership was being forged. No winners, no losers, just comrades.

14

The Promised Land

Mother sat under the poinciana tree in our yard working on a portrait of me. Since her portrait of the family, which she had framed and hung up in the sitting room, she had stopped drawing. The portrait took longer than she anticipated and she had developed a pain in her wrist. It had only recently got better and so she took up her charcoal and exercise book again. There I was, dressed up in a long-sleeved white shirt, long pants and black shoes. I sat on the scatter rug Granny Una had made, right elbow resting on an old cushion, left leg drawn up, the other streched out. I sat sideways reading *A Treasury of Jamaican Poetry*, which was lying open on the rug.

I wasn't sure whether I liked what I had seen so far: my legs were long, my arms were long; my fingers were long. In fact, my whole body seemed so long. I had grown so much. I didn't recognise myself. We didn't have a full-length mirror at home. Seeing the full extent of my body was strange: my hair was cropped close, my face was dark and smooth, my nose was wide, my right ear looked roundish, my mouth was slightly opened, my eyes were downcast. Felix had grown, but he was not as tall as me. He said the picture was the spitting image of me.

Felix was sketching, too. Aunt Isabelle had hung some of his sketches in the school and I was so proud of him. Felix had taken over where Mother left off. He liked to walk through the village on his own, sketching plant and animal life. His pictures were really good, even Janey, whom we called Miss Morris, had taken a few of them, so the children in her class could learn about the different insects to be found in the countryside. Felix's parents were really proud of him. People kept saying: 'Mas Rupee, yuh puppah lef' yuh wid a mountain o' debt, but 'im gran'pickney inherit de real legacy. Why, de bwoy can draw, just like him gran'puppah Chen used to.'

It was generally understood that Felix would take the JSC and Aunt Isabelle had promised to enquire about him going to the Jamaica School of Art. She was sure he'd be accepted because his pictures were first class. Aunt Isabelle was also interested in art. She had a newspaper clipping of a painting by a self-taught Jamaican artist called Mallica Reynolds, known as Kapo. The painting was called *Old Richmond*. It captured the different sizes and shapes of the houses in, we presumed, Old Richmond. The houses were perched on a hillside with lots of plant life but there was not a soul in sight. Felix had drawn a similar picture, called *Dwellings*. But he had included the villagers going about their daily routine.

Aunt Isabelle paid Felix one shilling for *Dwellings*. She was going to have the picture framed. When news leaked that Felix had earned money for drawing a picture, the parishioners said he was 'a talented boy'. He accepted their praise silently, for he would have preferred Aunt Hetty's blessing. Sadly, the people whose praise we both wanted had passed away.

'I'm going to keep all my sketches from now on,' Felix said. 'I want to rework them when I go to art school.'

Felix had a talent and I knew it. He could draw anything in sight. I said, 'What is my talent, Felix?'

Mother interrupted. She said: 'Festus, don't move. Talent is not something you can see or touch.' Then she added, 'Time for a break. We'll continue tomorrow.'

Felix said, 'Let's go and see Uncle Hyman, Festus. We haven't seen him for ages.'

Uncle Hyman was fishing as usual. He said: 'Bwoys, a 'ear yuh both mekin' a name fe yuhself: artist an' scholar.'

'Howdy-do, Uncle Hyman.' We hung our heads, feeling bashful. But soon we rolled up our trouser legs and twiddled our toes in the water, watching the red clay on the river-bed. The water was crystal clear. The fishing-rod began to jerk and Felix helped Uncle Hyman to reel in the catch.

'Oh no!' I said. There was an eel wriggling in the air.

'Yuh stray far from 'ome, eel.' Uncle Hyman turned to me. 'Festus, stop acting like frighten Friday, bwoy!'

Felix was busy examining the eel; he wanted to draw it. He said, 'As slippery as an eel.'

Uncle Hyman said: 'A thought yuh bwoys throw me weh. Long time a dohn see oono.' He threw the eel into the water. 'Safe journey home, frien'.'

We left Uncle Hyman whistling. Felix looked back at him, saying: 'That's a sad tune. It reminds me of long ago, when we first went to basic school: we used to crawl under the table, hiding from the teacher, and if one of us didn't have a pencil, the other would break his in half and share it.'

'Remember the time I broke my slate and shared it with you?'

'Granny Una bought that slate for you,' Felix said. 'She was really cross. Fancy breaking a brand-new slate in half.'

Felix and I parted company then, and I could still hear Uncle Hyman's faint whistling, so sad, in the distance.

Later my parents and I had supper with Aunt

Isabelle, who'd advised them on the day I passed the CEE to send me to America to study. My parents had missed the school concert because they had been to Kingston to see about getting me a passport. It was all taken care of and now they were talking about my date of departure. Aunt Isabelle had a sister in New York who would receive me.

'Well, Festus, you won't be here for much longer,' Aunt Isabelle said. 'My sister Eva has written to say her grandson Spencer is looking forward to making friends with you. You'll be going to the same high school.'

'I don't want to go to America. What about those race riots they've been having?'

Aunt Isabelle said seriously: 'According to the radio and the *Gleaner*, there's rioting in Kingston, Festus. The Black Power movement has reached Jamaica. Don't worry about race riots, Festus. Seize opportunity while you can.'

'That's right, son,' Father said. 'Many children would give their eyeteeth to be in your shoes.'

We were sitting on the verandah. Peeny-wallies buzzed around the gas lamp. Mother said, 'Stop worrying your little head about race riots, Festus. You are on a mission.'

The remainder of the evening was taken up with plans for my future. Aunt Isabelle had insisted on paying my keep. Mr Lloyd had left her well provided for and they had no children.

Janey Morris came out on to the verandah wearing a sleeveless, red shift. She said, 'Good evening, folks.'

We all said, 'Good evening, Janey.' Then Mother turned to Aunt Isabelle and said, 'Why don't you and Janey come to dinner on Sunday?'

Father said, 'Good idea.' Then he added, 'We'd better get going. I don't like leaving Mama on her own, not since she twisted her ankle the other day. And yesterday she complained of a pain in her chest. She says it's just gas. Who knows?'

We said goodnight. Then Father took out his flashlight and Aunt Isabelle said, 'Walk good.'

Nineteen sixty-eight was the year Felix and I had our twelfth birthday. It was to be a memorable year for so many reasons: the radio carried news that there were rioting and fatalities in Kingston when Professor Walter Rodney (a so-called political agitator) of the University of the West Indies was expelled from Jamaica. Martin Luther King was assassinated in Memphis, Tennessee, in April of that year. There were race riots all over America. I was afraid of leaving Jamaica, terrified of going to America. Mercifully, my passport took longer than we had anticipated and I was pleased about the delay. I didn't want to leave my family, and sometimes I found myself looking into space, fretting. I hated the thought of not seeing Felix again, hated the thought of going away. The school holidays drew to a close and my departure drew nigh.

It was countdown time and Felix was allowed to sleep over at my house every other night; I did likewise at his house. One morning we stood on the verandah at my house, admiring Felix's sketch of Aunt Vanda's cottage with two birds perched on the roof: *The Rooks*, he called it. Felix had sketched the pets of all the old people whom we used to visit: there was one sketch of rabbits in a hutch; Aunt Kizzy's rabbits. There was another of pigs in a sty; Aunt Agatha's pigs. There was one of Uncle Hyman reeling in an eel. There was even a sketch of the men in the village square, crouching outside Uncle Caesar's shop as if they were jockeys riding horses.

Granny Una greeted us. 'Marnin' Bwoys.' She had not been well for some time. She complained of a pain in her chest. Her ankle was still swollen. She used Aunt Hetty's walking-stick now.

'We're going up to Aunt Hetty's house today, Granny,' I said. 'Would you like to come? We're going to write our names and the date on the banyan tree.'

Mother came out on to the verandah, saying, 'Boys, give Matilda my love.'

Granny Una said, 'Even if yuh hadn't asked, a would a still come. A want fe see how Matilda is. A can't wait fe deliver de nex' baby.'

Matilda was expecting her second child any time now. Granny Una visited her often, saying Matilda needed company in the daytime since Osman was busy cultivating the land. In truth, Granny Una loved listening to the parakeets; she loved the banyan tree, too. It reminded her of the old days when she and Grandpa Cuffee used to dance the quadrille.

It was way past eleven o'clock when we set off. Felix and I picked the bitter cerasee fruits along the path and sucked them. The bees and wasps buzzed around the daisies. Granny Una walked with the help of her walking-stick. The sun was beating down on our heads as usual. We could see the heat shimmering high on the hillside. Felix and I stopped now and then, picking buttercups, looking at the jagged stones and the coconut trees littering the hillside.

'Tan tuddy.' Granny Una pointed her stick. 'Bwoys, is who dat man standin' in me way. Wat a way 'im remin' me of me dear . . .' All of a sudden she dropped the walking-stick and hugged her cardigan to her chest, saying, 'Lawd, dis pain gwine kill me. Gimme a 'and, Festus.'

'I'm coming, Granny.' I ran. 'I'm coming.'

Right there along the path, Granny Una went down on her knees, as though in prayer. She hit her knees on a rock.

'Hold on, Granny.' I reached out to her.

'Get Matilda, Felix,' Granny Una groaned. 'Run, run . . .'

I sat on a stone, resting Granny Una's head in my lap. Then she just flopped down. 'Oh Lord,' I wailed. 'Oh Lord!'

We were high above the village and sound travelled. Felix ran up the path, hollering: 'Help, help; Granny Una's dying!' His voice was carried far below us.

'Dear Lord, please don't take Granny away.' I rocked her.

Uncle Caesar came riding up the hill on his horse, Fagan. He had been riding in the opposite direction, on his debt-collecting rounds. He dismounted and flung himself down at Granny Una's side, saying: 'What's the matter, Mama?'

She opened her eyes. 'Pain eena me 'eart, Caesar, pain.'

'It's just gas, Granny,' I said. 'You told me so yourself the other day. You've got the same complaint as Missis Leena.'

'No, Festus,' she said. 'Me time come, chile, Dat was Cuffee standin' in de path ahead. My dear Cuffee com' fe meet me. Dohn cry, chile; dohn cry.'

'What are you saying, Mama?' Uncle Caesar asked.

'A see Cuffee standin' up ahead,' Granny Una said. 'Yuh know spirits always come fe guide loved ones home, son.'

'No, Granny,' I said. 'It was a mirage. That's all.'

'God bless yuh, Festus,' she said. 'Be a good boy an' kiss yuh granny goodbye.'

My tears fell on her face. 'I want you to live, Granny,' I said. 'I want you to live . . .'

Matilda came down the path carrying Joy on her hip. Her stomach was so large she couldn't bend down. She stood there sobbing: 'I don't want you to die, Granny . . .'

Granny Una tried to hold up her head, but she couldn't. I held it up for her. Then she said, 'De road is rocky, Matty. Yuh mus' get we MP fe do something 'bout it.'

Matilda did not reply. She just stood there clinging to Joy, looking awkward because she couldn't bend down.

'Felix, come and kiss yuh granny, chile,' Granny Una said.

For a moment Felix hesitated. Then he bent, weeping.

'Caesar,' Granny Una said, 'please tek me 'ome, son.'

'No, Granny,' Matilda said. 'It's dangerous to move you. Come up to my place.'

Granny Una groaned: 'Me bed, Caesar; me bed . . . Please.'

Felix's cry had aroused the villagers. A large crowd came up the hill, even the unemployed men who sat on the shop piazza. People stood with their arms folded, gaping, not knowing what to say. Then Mother and Father came.

'Granny Una had a heart attack, Father,' Matilda said.

Father wailed, 'Mama dead without saying goodbye to me. Mama, oh! Mama, oh!'

Granny Una opened her eyes and said slowly: 'Salvan, yuh tryin' fe wake de dead or suppen? Hush, chile, hush.'

Father fell on his knees and kissed her forehead. 'You're going to be all right, Mama; you're going . . .'

But even as he kissed her he knew she was on her

'way to Canaan land'. Her weight bore down on me and it was ten times worse than the weight I felt on the morning of the CEE. Granny Una had gone and died on me, just like that.

'Lawd a macy,' Missis Leena said. 'Do Rupee, catch Felix. De chile faint weh!'

There was a loud 'boof': Felix had fallen, fainted away. Mas Rupee carried him like a baby down the path with Missis Leena following. Father and Uncle Caesar lifted the dead weight of Granny Una's body, freeing my legs. But when I stood up my legs were so weak I couldn't support myself.

'Use Granny's walking-stick, Festus,' Matilda said.

Mother took my arm, and I steadied myself with the walking-stick. In that moment I was an old man walking down the path, walking past the solemn-looking villagers who made way for us.

The funeral touched the hearts of many. Granny Una was buried in the family plot. As we stood in the burial ground where Grandpa Cuffee slept in peace, I noticed the graves stretching back in time: Grandpa Cuffee's parents, his brothers, even a sister, and babies, too. It was frightening to see your family tree, the branches all resting in peace. There I stood, Felix by my side, listening to the pastor reading Psalm 27, saying: ' . . .Wait on the Lord: be of good courage, and he shall strengthen thine heart . . .' Then we all sang, 'When the saints go marching in . . .'

Granny Una's favourite Bible passage was the story of Ruth and Naomi. Mother read from the Book of Ruth, reciting: 'And Ruth said, Entreat me not to leave thee, or to return from following thee: for wither thou goest, I will go; and where thou lodgest, I will lodge . . . Where thou diest, will I die, and there will I be buried . . .'

Barnaby broke down then. He flung himself across

the coffin and sobbed: 'Take me with you, Granny. Take me . . .'

When Barnaby was very young he used to beg Granny Una to take him to the market with her. She often did. Also, when he misbehaved as a child, Father would take out the rod and Barnaby would run straight under Granny Una's bed, crying. She would beg mercy for him then. Now his voice sounded childlike, as if he'd reverted to childhood. Mother remembered, too: she burst into tears and clung to Father who was also crying.

Missie Leena, who had neither mother nor father, had looked on Granny Una as a surrogate mother. She and Mas Rupee wept openly. They were too upset to restrain Barnaby. Osman had stayed home with Joy and Matilda, who had taken to bed since Granny Una's death. It was Janey who said: 'Come, Barnaby, come . . .' She slipped an arm round his waist, and the funeral proceeded.

The morning of my departure coincided with Granny Una's wake, nine days after the funeral. It was impossible to cancel my flight. Who would have expected Granny Una to die so suddenly? I couldn't believe I would be journeying into the unknown on the same day my granny was making her homeward-bound journey.

Aunt Isabelle had come to see me off. Janey came, too. Matilda had given birth on the day after the funeral. She now had a baby boy named Moses. The yard was full of people. You would have thought it was Matilda's wedding all over again. But there was no rejoicing. People had come to spend the whole day. This set-up would be a twenty-four hour affair: everyone brought food and drink. My parents provided nothing.

The pastor said: 'Festus, it's a hard road to travel

and a mighty long way to go; ask Jesus to be your guide.'

The post mistress said: 'Festus, I'm looking forward to seeing all those airmail letters, keep me busy.'

'Oh, Father,' I cried, 'please don't send me away. Can't I go to high school in Town? I'm frightened. I don't want to be alone, not now. I'm scared.' Everyone was listening.

It was Missis Leena who said, 'Yuh mus' go, Festus. Wat would Mama say? Yuh dohn want fe let yuh granny dung, do yuh?'

Matilda and Osman said, 'We'll all be able to hold our heads up if you go, Festus; same way you held up Granny's head before she died.' Matilda cradled Moses. Osman cuddled Joy.

'Papa,' Felix said, 'please beg Mas Salvan not to let Festus go. He's going to be so lonely without us.'

Aunt Isabelle said: 'Festus, you must go. Your talent lies in reading and writing. Go and finish your education.'

The twins, Marigold and Primrose, stepped forward. They were tall and lean now. They wore yellow sleeveless shifts and black pumps. They said, 'We are going to take the CEE next year, Festus. We hope we'll be as successful as you.'

'I am not successful,' I said to myself. 'I am going into exile.' Instead I said aloud, 'Good luck to both of you.'

The poinciana tree was in bloom again. The red blossoms had turned brown. A thought occurred to me. I said, 'Felix, you've drawn everything but the poinciana tree.'

'I'll send it to you,' he said. 'I promise.'

'I'll write every day, Felix,' I said. 'I promise.'

Uncle Caesar and Aunt Esther came. They said, 'Festus, you won't be travelling through the valley of the shadow of death alone; Granny Una will be your guide.'

Felix clung to me and cried, 'I don't want you to go, Festus. What if they kill you, just like Martin Luther King?'

'Come, come, Felix,' Mas Rupee said. 'Let Festus go. He must travel that lonesome valley alone.'

Mother was wearing a new pinafore. It sat just below the knee, making her look much younger. She and Father hugged and kissed me. They said, 'You are carrying the banner for the whole family, Festus. But if you look close enough you will see the word "Love" written all over it. We love you, son. Never forget that.'

Barnaby patted me on the back. 'Well, Festus, what will you be: lawyer, doctor, Syrian, chief?' That was all he said.

I did not know what to say. I stood there feeling as if my heart would split asunder. It thumped in my chest. I just wanted the safety of my bed, in the same way Granny Una had begged for the safety of hers. I felt as if a part of me had died that day on the hillside. So many people were counting on me, especially those who had passed away. I pulled myself together and said, 'I'm ready now.'

Busha, the overseer of York Castle was waiting. He had surprised everyone by proposing to Aunt Rachel at Granny Una's funeral. They saw each other every day now because they had been made caretakers of the great house. He had offered to drive me to Palisadoes airport and my parents had accepted eagerly. He said, 'Festus, no baddah com' back to Jamaica wid noh American twang, bwoy.'

Uncle Hyman had borrowed Granny Una's walking-stick. His shoulders were hunched up overnight. He said: 'Festus, dem cast yuh adrift eena de wilderness, bwoy. Neber fear; wheneber yuh feel afraid, jus' whistle a 'appy tune.'

Father double-checked the tag on my grip. Mother held my passport. She hugged me. 'Now is the hour, Festus. Study hard and come home with a first-class degree, son.'

'Yes, Mother,' I said. But I didn't really care about a degree then. I just wanted the safety of home.

Felix said: '*Vamoose*, Festus; off you go.'

I adopted Mr Lloyd's tone, 'Adiós, amigo!'

Busha climbed into the Land Rover, tooting the horn. My parents followed him. I stood by the vehicle, lips quivering. Suddenly, Mas Rupee, Missis Leena and Felix were upon me.

'Festus, bwoy,' Mas Rupee said, 'yuh neber t'ink seh we would let yuh go all de way to Palisadoes widout company, eh?'

The Land Rover was built for passengers: Father sat up front with Busha. Mother, Missis Leena and Mas Rupee sat in the middle section. Felix and I sat at the back, sharing the first part of my journey into exile. We looked out the window, waving at the crowd as if we were both going away.

The hurricane season was over the horizon. The clouds had been gathering all week. As we headed in the direction of Clarendon, there was a loud 'bdoi, bdoi!' Thunder clapped and lightning flashed. Busha swerved his body with the Land Rover, saying: 'Bwoy, de road rocky, sah. Time Mr Mullings, our MP, do sinting 'bout it.'

Next minute lightning flashed and the rain came tunmbling down. Missis Leena said, 'Massah God open de windows of 'eaven. Looks like de angels cryin', sah!'

Our parents sang, 'Oh children, don't you weep, don't you mourn . . . We shall overcome some day . . .'

For a split second I wondered whether they were referring to the angels weeping or Felix and myself. Then I thought of the villagers running for shelter out of the rain. Would there be enough room in our house for them? No. I thought of Granny Una, too. Would there be room in heaven for her? Yes. Perhaps that's why God had opened the doors. Lightning flashed across the windscreen. Felix and I leaned on each other, afraid of the thunder and lightning and the future. How could we not weep when we were about to go separate ways? So say, so done: our tears flowed in unison with the rain.

Glossary

Creole	English
Afu	Species of yam
Backra/Bakra	White person of planter class
Bankra	Wicker basket
Baddah	Bother
Baas	Sir
Big chat	Loud mouth
Boasty-bwoy	Show off
Botheration	Trouble
Bredda/ brodda/s	Brother/s
Bruk	Break
Buck up	Bump into
But see yah	Look/see here
Bwoy/s	Boy/s
Cassava Pone	Pudding
Chi-chi bud	Long-tail bird
Cho-cho	Vegetable
Cous	Cousin
Cuffee	Ghanian name for a man born on Friday
Dokono	Cornmeal pudding
Dose	Those
Dung	Down
Duppy/ies	Ghost/s
Duppy-man	Male ghost
Eena	In
Fallah	Follow

Fe	To
Fe/Fi	For
Fo-fool	Simple/silly
Gwane	Go on
Gwine	Going
Jab/s	Job/s
Jamma	Work song
Haffe	Have to
Lawd a macy	Lord have mercy
Let 'er ears eat grass	Leave her alone
Li'k/lick	Hit
Lite	Light
Macy	Mercy
Maddy-maddy	Mad/insane
Mek-mek	Grumble
Mek we dip . . .	Let us dip . . .
'Memba	Remember
Merino	Vest
Mumma/h	Mother
Nayga	Negro
Neber	Never
Negya	Negro
Nuh	Don't
Nyam	Eat quickly
Ooman	Woman
Oono	You
Patchy-patchy	Blotches
Peeny-wally/ies	Firefly/ies
Pickney/s	Child/children
Puppa/h	Father
Puttin' pressure 'pon we 'ead	Fretting/mourning
Red-eye	Envious
Rolling-calf	Evil spirit
Sah	Sir

Shine-yeye	Demanding/envious
Siddung	Sit down
Silly-silly	Silly
Smaddy	Somebody
Stan' me groun'	Stood still
Stoshus	Classy/smart
Suppen	Something
Sweet-mouth	Flattery
Tan tuddy	Stand still
Taut	Thought
Tedday	Today
'Tep	Step
Throw me weh	Forgotten me
Tony-C	Quiff
Tumble dung	Fell over
Twang	Accent
Wahn	Want
Weh	What/where
Weh	Away
Wo'd	Words
Wo'k	Work
Yeye	Eye